What the critics are saying...

Always Faithful

"If you enjoy delving deeply into the personal lives of a lusty you couple, ALWAYS FAITHFUL may be just the book you're looking for." ~ *Jani Brooks, Romance Today*

"Readers will enjoy this story of a sexy yet sensitive man in uniform and the woman that loves him." ~ *Miriam van Veen, Love Romances*

"Alli Nicole had written a story with intriguing characters that draw you in a charming tale of love. The characters are loveable and sexy and the sex scenes are steamy. You need to read ALWAYS FAITHFUL as this story is incredible and will transport you into the military life. Ladies, you will not want to leave your man in uniform." ~ *Karen, Love Romance*

One of the Few

"WOW!!! This was an awesome story. It grabbed my interest right from the beginning and held it until I turned the last page. This is one of those stories that won't let you put it down and have you feeding your kids cold cereal for dinner. Hey, kids love Lucky Charms right? I highly recommend this to anyone who loves to read sensual romance." ~*Beatrice Sigman, The Best Reviews*

"The sexual tension and build up between Boothe and Roxie sizzles. When they do finally make love these two set the pages on fire. ONE OF THE FEW by Alli Nicole has a solid storyline, a super sexy hero and a very sensual romance." ~ *Tami Sutton, Escape to Romance*

LUST IN UNIFORM

By Allie Nicole

Lust in Uniform
An Ellora's Cave Publication, January 2005

Ellora's Cave Publishing, Inc.
1337 Commerce Drive
Stow, Ohio 44224

ISBN #1419951254

Edited by: Ann Richardson
Cover art by: Syneca

Warning:

The following material contains graphic sexual content meant for mature readers. *Lust in Uniform* has been rated *E-rotic* by a minimum of three independent reviewers.

Ellora's Cave Publishing offers three levels of Romantica™ reading entertainment: S (S-ensuous), E (E-rotic), and X (X-treme).

S-*ensuous* love scenes are explicit and leave nothing to the imagination.

E-*rotic* love scenes are explicit, leave nothing to the imagination, and are high in volume per the overall word count. In addition, some E-rated titles might contain fantasy material that some readers find objectionable, such as bondage, submission, same sex encounters, forced seductions, etc. E-rated titles are the most graphic titles we carry; it is common, for instance, for an author to use words such as "fucking", "cock", "pussy", etc., within their work of literature.

X-*treme* titles differ from E-rated titles only in plot premise and storyline execution. Unlike E-rated titles, stories designated with the letter X tend to contain controversial subject matter not for the faint of heart.

LUST IN UNIFORM

ALWAYS FAITHFUL
&
ONE OF THE FEW

Alli Nicole

ALWAYS FAITHFUL

Dedication

Thanks to our husbands who supported our dreams, our gracious friends and family for giving us our first critiques, and our children and grandchildren who understood when we needed time to write.

A special thanks to the United States Marine Corps for their part in fighting for our country.

Thanks to Kurt Pedersen, Sgt. USMC, and the Desert Storm Community Forum for sharing their experiences.

Prologue

For Nikki Phillips, stepping aboard the non-stop British Air flight to London seemed the toughest decision of her twenty-two years of life. Nikki had developed into a self-sufficient, headstrong young woman from her parents rearing. Her last relationship left her drained of self-confidence and vulnerable. However, determined to regain her independence, Nikki left the States to start anew in her mother's homeland. Her goal consisted of finding the woman she'd lost and making her a success.

Brandon's attention had captivated her. His masculine beauty touched with slight arrogance kept her interested. His constant selfishness finally sent her packing. Nikki tolerated his belittlement and verbal abuse for their few months together. Why? She couldn't quite put her finger on it. Possibly the thought of having no boyfriend outweighed the thought of being miserable with one.

Brandon attempted to control her every move, dictating what she wore, what she did, and who her friends were. He'd convinced her that she would do as he asked if she loved him. Unfortunately, she'd fallen into his trap. *I will not let that happen again,* she told herself.

After graduating from the University of Texas, Nikki secured a job as a systems engineer for the government. She could leave the baggage behind her in Texas. No more excuses. No man telling her what she should do. This time, she controlled her own mind. She left knowing the strength she once lost could be found by doing so. She took the leap of faith with no safety net.

Chapter One

"Why don't you just loosen up," Brandon said to her as he savagely began unbuttoning her blouse. "You know you want to. All women want it, they just don't admit it."

"I just don't feel like it, that's all," Nikki told him trying to push him away from her. This task was next to impossible in the compact front seat of his Chevy Camaro. "Why do you always want to do it in the car anyway?"

"It's dangerous. There is always that chance of getting caught again."

Nikki looked out the window to the empty field in front of them. The dead end street, now christened "their hideaway," the place Brandon could get his rocks off.

Nikki remembered the mortification she felt the last time they parked there. Both of them lay naked as two jaybirds finishing the dirty deed, when a bright light shone into the passenger side window on them. Brandon thought it hilarious as he pulled his pants up quickly and got out of the car to speak to the officer. Nikki hurriedly refastened her bra and pulled up her pants as the flashlight still beamed in on her nakedness.

Couldn't he turn that damn thing off? Lord knows he should have gotten his thrills by now, she thought to herself.

Nikki grew increasingly pissed off the longer Brandon stood outside the car shooting the shit with Barney Fife.

"He said that we need to find a safer place next time I want to get in your pants," Brandon said still giggling when he got back into the car.

"I am not going to do it here," Nikki said coming back to the present. "I don't want to have to face my daddy when he has to bail me out for indecent exposure."

"You are such a prude," Brandon said as he removed his member from his pants and began readying himself for invasion.

God, she hated having sex with him. He couldn't care less about her feelings. Surely sex supplied more than just wham, bam, thank-you, ma'am. But Brandon sure didn't possess that knowledge. Nikki always felt so used, so manipulated, so unappreciated. Something about him kept pulling her in. There were times he made her feel special. However, looking back she realized it was only the times that sexual satisfaction consumed him. Surely, being in love provided more contentment than she felt now.

"Fine, if you're not going to pleasure me, then I'll just have to do it myself," Brandon said as he began bringing himself to satisfaction.

A lump grew in Nikki's throat. She swallowed hard attempting to avoid the urge to throw up. Totally disgusted, she looked away as he continued to slide his hand up and down his arousal. She tried to block out the sounds of his moans of release.

"If you're finished, I'd like to go back to the dorm."

"Whatever."

When he pulled into the parking lot at the University he reached across and squeezed her breast and smiled, "So, can I come up?"

Nikki restrained the rage rising up in her chest. "Look, you bastard. I don't want to ever see you again. You are the most disgusting person I have ever met. I can't believe I have wasted so much time being your harlot. You obviously don't need me anymore since you seem so fond of your right hand. Besides, I know that if that doesn't do it, you can call that chick from our English Lit class who I know you've been screwing on the sly."

Brandon shook his head in disbelief. "How did you—Well, if you knew how to treat a guy, I wouldn't have to go to anyone else."

"You are a son of a bitch, Brandon. Why don't you just go to hell?"

That night proved to be the last time she saw Brandon on any kind of intimate basis. Shortly after that night, they graduated. She left for England. Brandon would eventually find his way into some other poor, sad, stupid woman's pants; and Nikki swore on all that she held sacred to never suffer men again, at least not in the foreseeable future.

✳ ✳ ✳ ✳ ✳

"Where to, Miss?" said the expressionless British cabby as he glanced at her through the rear divider of the taxi.

"Hampsthwaite, please."

13

The cab smelled of smoke and greasy food, and the cabby looked as if he consumed plenty of both on a regular basis. She held on tightly to the door strap as the cabby quickly weaved in and out of traffic during the twenty-minute ride into the village. That last turn, undoubtedly, he took on only two wheels.

The countryside of North Yorkshire fascinated Nikki. The green pastures and purple heather rushed quickly by the window. She loved the look of the craggy hills and winding roads. She directed the driver. The driver carefully entered the narrow stone and wood gate and approached 28 Hollins Lane, a small cottage typical of the area.

Rosebushes and flowerbeds surrounded the house. Construction of the cottage was of a dark local stone tinged slightly dark green. The dark stones bordered with white wooden trim lent a picture postcard appearance to the cottage. Glass bricks framed the dark green front door. Nikki sighed with approval as she made her way up the steps.

With no small effort, the aging and overweight cabby extracted himself from the cockpit of his cab, shuffled around, pulled out her luggage and carried it to the small front porch.

"Two fifty, Miss," the driver mumbled as he turned back to Nikki.

Nikki pulled out her wallet and handed the cabby the coins.

"Ta love," he mumbled.

Even in August, the bite of the northern wind that trekked down the valley stung her nose. She knew that back in Texas her family endured one hundred degree temperatures about now. Although only sixteen hours ago Nikki had been enjoying the high temperatures, it seemed more like months.

She welcomed the change in climate. However, the drizzle was another issue altogether. A frown spread over her face when the kink seized her naturally curly hair.

Nikki retrieved the front door key, from the pre-designated rock, and opened the door leading to the narrow spiral staircase. She walked through the entryway and into the den. The fireplace welcomed her and Nikki observed the abundance of kindling and coal left in the wood box by the landlord.

"Bless you, Mr. Dawson," she said to herself.

French doors separated the den from the patio, complimenting the beautiful picture window across the room. Nikki stumbled on a fleece blanket, spread over the furnished sofa, and gathered it up swiftly. She then snuggled up to tour the rest of the house.

The kitchen appeared small, but efficient. Nikki snickered when she noticed the piggyback washer and dryer by the small door leading to the backyard. They held a spooky likeness to the appliances Barbie possessed in her Dream House.

As she entered the dining room, Nikki ran her fingers along the antique buffet that complimented a small pine table and chairs. The draft, from the large bay window, made her spine tingle as she looked through to the flower garden and tool shed out back. She spotted the rooftops of the houses behind hers and inhaled deeply the aroma floating from the chimneys. Laying the blanket back on the sofa, she grabbed her luggage and meandered upstairs to unpack.

The exquisite bedroom consisted of a small table and chairs, four-poster bed and a beautiful armoire. The bed displayed crisp white sheets under a fluffy down duvet she imagined crawling under and wrapping herself in oblivion. The windowed wall offered a detailed view of the village. Looking out, Nikki could see the houses stair-stepping down the lane and ending at a small stone bridge. All *very quaint*, she thought to herself.

Nikki spent two hours unpacking most of her belongings, until exhaustion finally took her. She put on her flannel pajamas and crawled underneath the down comforter pulling it just under her nose. A sigh of ecstasy escaped her as she hunkered down lower in the bed. No longer able to contain herself, Nikki squealed with delight, flailing her legs under the covers.

"I'm free!" she whispered before the heavy hand of slumber overtook her.

Chapter Two

Nikki woke the next morning to the dull plunking sound of rainfall hitting the clay tile. Flinging her legs over the edge of the bed, she yawned and stretched her arms above her head. Her toes curled from the chill of the bare floor as she stood.

Looking out the window, she could see women of the village pulling their two-wheeled grocery carts behind them, fully reminiscent of ancient golfers trudging through the morning drizzle and seemingly ignoring it. She decided to disregard the nuisance as well and take a walk through the small village bordering her cottage.

Nikki pulled on her jeans, sweater, roper style boots and the obligatory waterproof jacket before heading down the front steps and out the gate. On the right, just past the cottage, there stood a quaint Protestant church with ivy and algae vying equally for living space on the ancient stonewall.

She continued down the cobblestone walkway noticing a corner store cum post office counter on the corner. She bought some local postcards and stamps to notify her family she did, indeed, arrive safely. At the dead end intersection of her lane sat a neighborhood pub, open, and serving lunch.

The sign above the entrance read, *Joiner Arms*. Nikki decided the pub sounded fabulous for lunch, and perhaps she would meet some of her neighbors. Her stomach grumbled in agreement with the idea of having lunch. The last meal she remembered consisted of the 'delectable' rubbery chicken she had consumed on the airplane, yesterday.

She opened the door to the smell of cooking food and instantly invoked a second rumbling from her stomach.

"Yummm," she said.

Nikki hopped on the nearest barstool and offered the bartender her most friendly smile. The emanation of ale drifted by her as the ruggedly handsome bartender performed the ritual of wiping down the dark mahogany bar in front of her.

"What'll it be, Miss?"

"What's that I smell?" Nikki asked.

"The house special, Nettie's fish and chips."

"Oh, that sounds great. I haven't had good fish and chips in years."

"Can I bring you something while you wait?"

"How about a pint?" she said looking around the pub.

The bartender started to turn for a glass, then twisted back abruptly. "You a Yank?" he asked.

Nikki's head straightened and with a little ice in her voice responded, "No, I am not a Yank!"

"You talk like a Yank," the bartender said smiling.

"I'm American if that's what you mean," Nikki said irritably.

"Yea, a Yank." The bartender let out a chuckle.

"A Yank is someone who lives north of the Mason-Dixon Line. I'm from Texas and that is south. People in the south don't like being called Yanks!"

"Sorry, Tex. You got a ranch?" he replied with a British accented Texas drawl. Obviously, he watched the old *Dallas* TV series.

Nikki couldn't help but smile. "No, nor any oil wells." They both laughed then as he pulled her beer.

"Are you visiting someone?"

"Nope, I live here. I'm renting the Dawson House down the road. Mr. Dawson is an old friend of my parents. I'm staying there until I get my own place."

"Well, I guess we'll be seeing a lot of you around the village, eh? My name is Ian Canterbury." He held out his hand to shake hers.

"I'm Nikki Phillips," she said as she took his hand in hers. Nikki wolfed down the fish and chips and drank the beer. The meal sated her taste buds. "My compliments to the chef," she said.

"Well, you might as well meet the chef. Nettie," he called. "Your presence is required."

A woman only slightly shorter than Ian emerged from behind the wall separating the kitchen from the main room.

"You bellowed, Oh Great One?" she asked.

"Here now, none of your sass in front of the paying customers," he smiled broadly.

"This young lady has come all the way from the wild plains of Texas to sample your cuisine."

"Nikki, meet Nettie. Nikki's down the lane in John Dawson's place," Ian stated as he patted Nettie on the shoulder. "She has nothing but praise for your fish and chips."

"Pay no attention to this lout, love." Nettie extended her hand but only after wiping it with the bar towel threaded through her apron sash. "I'm pleased to meet you, Nikki." Nettie spotted a customer signaling for attention down the bar and said, "Must run. Ta, love. Please come back," and she took off.

After paying Ian and taking her leave of him, she turned to head out of the door. However, before she could stop, she smashed her nose into a brick wall and slipped awkwardly to the floor, landing on her backside. After her initial astonishment subsided, she looked up into the face of a very tall and handsome man. Only then did she realize the "brick wall" consisted of his obviously well-muscled chest.

Will Chambers noticed Nikki the instant she entered the pub and quickly elbowed his friend, Boothe O'Brien, sitting next to him. He continued to watch her mannerisms while she ate and drank her pint. Her long wavy hair fell just past her shoulders. Will fantasized how silky the black locks might feel between his fingers. Her shapely long legs led to a firm, but full derriere. He smiled then, thinking that he liked his women with a little meat on their bones.

Her breasts offered a bit more than a handful and were perfectly proportional to the rest of her. Her slender neck led to a stubborn jaw displaying the sensuous pout of her mouth. Her full cheeks gave her an expression of girlish innocence. Her blue-green, or maybe green-blue eyes pierced through him. *Aqua*, Will thought to himself. Probably the type of color capable of subtly altering depending on what colors she wore. Simple irresistibility poured from every pore of her skin.

"Damn!" Nikki stammered trying quickly to regain her composure. "I'm so sorry," she said looking directly into Will's deep blue eyes.

"It was entirely my pleasure, ma'am," he said in what sounded to be an exaggerated southern drawl. Will held his hand out to her offering assistance.

"Oh, aren't you funny?" she said brushing the proffered hand away and standing on her own.

"What's funny?" he said in the same drawl.

"You don't need to make fun of my accent," Nikki said icily as she brushed the crumbs from her backside.

Will turned toward his snickering friend behind him.

"Boothe, it looks like we met us a fellow southerner. I'm from Fort Worth, darlin'," he said as he turned to face her again.

"Darlin'? I'm not your *darlin'*!" she sneered at him.

He noticed the anger in her eyes and quickly said, "Really, no fooling," and placed his right hand over his heart.

Nikki still remained doubtful, but softened her voice and said, "What are you two doing here?" Only after she said it did she realize that it sounded more accusatory than she intended.

His gaze slowly turned into a stare that made her ashamed of her outburst. She returned his stare and quickly evaluated his features. His bronze skin implied some Spanish heritage in his background. A firm, square jaw and eyelashes that most women would kill for, accented his deep blue eyes. His eyes held her entranced.

"Look, I'm sorry I snapped at you. I guess I'm still suffering from jet lag and I'm a bit grumpy," she said to him.

"It's okay, Darlin'. I'm just surprised to meet someone from the old neighborhood, so to speak. We're stationed here. I've been in England for over a year and except for Boothe here—he's from Atlanta—this is the first time I've met someone like you. From Texas, I mean."

When he spoke, she stepped back to acquire a more complete look at the rest of him. His severe flat top she recognized as that of a Marine. Her dad called it a *high and tight* cut. Growing up with a Marine father, she could spot one among a crowd of servicemen. Only Marines boasted that look about them.

She noticed the dark, curly hairs peeking over the top of his v-neck sweater. Very tight jeans she noticed extended tightly over muscular calves and firm thighs. Her eyes followed the curve of his legs and stopped abruptly at the bulge between his thighs. *Nice package,* she thought to herself. As her eyes approached his feet she chuckled. *Cowboy boots, Ropers, no less.*

"I'm from Fort Worth, too," Nikki finally said.

"Well, I guess you really are from the old neighborhood. And now we're neighbors in two countries."

"What do you mean?"

"I live next to the Dawson House." His unwavering gaze shook her.

Normally, Nikki knew how to conduct herself. Without question, this man made her nervous. She immediately put her shields up. No matter how gorgeous the man appeared, Nikki vowed to make no sexual instigations. Her eyes certainly enjoyed the sight of him. But, in her experience, with beauty comes vanity.

If her daddy had taught her nothing else, it was that she could do anything she wanted to, on her own. A husband was only an option. Although, she knew that this word of advice came only from a father who didn't want to admit that it scared him shitless to think about losing his only daughter to another man.

"Well, I guess I'll be seeing you," said Nikki.

"I reckon so," Will replied slowly.

Will smiled as he watched her walk out of the pub.

"I think I make her a might nervous. What do you think, Boothe?" he asked his friend.

"Yea, I'd say. The little thing's headlights were on bright from the start," Boothe said, referring to her hard nipples pressing against her shirt. He dodged the expected swat to the head Will projected at him.

Will tried not to notice that the hand he slapped Boothe with trembled slightly.

Her body made his heart race. She swiveled slightly when she walked down the street. He wanted to grab that cute little butt, but restrained himself. He'd let her go today, but he was definitely up for a chase.

Nikki left the pub feeling like an idiot. She probably sounded like an enamored little schoolgirl. Nikki didn't know how to react the next time she saw him. Unfortunately, seeing him again was inevitable considering he lived next door.

What did she care? She didn't want to get involved with any man. Remember?! But, damned if he didn't look good enough to eat! Only then did she realize that she didn't even know the man's name and laughed at herself.

"You'd better get your tongue back in your mouth before she turns around and sets fire to it. I don't mind saying it Will, that chick scares the hell out of me," Boothe said.

"Was it just me or was she just about the finest looking chick we've seen around here?" Will said not taking his eyes off her.

"She is fine looking. But let's face it she's mean as a junkyard dog! You haven't been screwed in, well, damn boy, how long has it been since you got your ashes hauled? She probably has guys like you for lunch. If you did get to her, you probably wouldn't be able to walk for days." Boothe said kiddingly.

"Boothe, you are a piece of work, you know that? There's more to life than getting laid."

"Not for me," Boothe said smirking.

"There's something about her, man. I can't put my finger on it. I wouldn't mind seeing her again."

"Yeah, like through her window when she's undressing and pray to God that she don't catch your ass."

"Boothe, have I ever told you that you're a pig?"

"Not lately," Boothe stated proudly.

Nikki kept walking even though she could feel the heat from their stares on her back. *Don't turn around, Nikki. Whatever you do, don't turn around.*

Wiggling her rear just a little bit more, she continued down the lane to her house. *Here, take that you military pukes, because that's all you're going to get!*

✳ ✳ ✳ ✳ ✳

Pilots don't see the faces. Artillery units are distanced from the violence. The infantry looks death straight in the eye.

Will's infantry unit came upon an Iraqi tank in one of the many ditches along the desert. The Iraqis built the ditches to hinder the enemy, but they caused just as much destruction to their own forces. The crew was long gone, with the exception of the driver of the tank. Will breathed deeply as he was consumed by the stench of death inside the compartment.

The inside of the Iraqi's legs were caked with blood where he impacted the steering wheel. Apparently, he was stretching upward to allow himself to see out of the driver's hatch. The top of the Iraqi's head peeled back like a can of sardines where flesh met steel.

Will's breathing quickened as the stench turned his stomach over. He jumped from the tank just in time to lose the meager portion of food that sat in his stomach. Sweat burned his eyes as he wiped his mouth on his sleeve in an attempt to regain control of his heaving.

Will woke up from the nightmare drenched and his heart pounding in his chest. The memories of war are rough on a Marine's sleep. Lying back down, throwing his arm over his eyes, he worked to bring his breathing back down. He sat on the side of the bed debating on a shot of whiskey or a cup of coffee to soothe him. With a slight grin he remembered a wiggling backside as it disappeared down a street and seemed to toss a challenge his way. His mom would love this little lady's spunk.

Chapter Three

At the sound of clinking glass, Nikki glanced out of the window past the sheer curtains and spotted Will coming out his front door to gather up his morning milk delivery. *Oh…my…God*, she thought.

He'd donned plaid flannel pants and nothing else. Her stomach tightened with the notion of running her fingers through the patch of hair adorning his well-defined chest! He stood up and stretched, breathing deeply to take in the fresh morning air. Unfortunately, the air held the aroma of the morning *mucking* from the surrounding pastures. Nikki laughed as Will scrunched up his nose in disgust.

He turned to go inside and she perceived the acute definition of the muscles in his back. She imagined how smooth they would feel under her fingers. Obviously, he religiously participated in the Corps mandated physical fitness standards.

When he closed his front door, she plopped down in her chair feeling the telling dampness between her legs. *What was she doing? She was no better than a Peeping Tom. But, God, he's incredible. It's only a physical attraction. She did not have time for a man. He probably has a girlfriend anyway. Maybe he's married. Did he have a ring on his finger the other day? Damn! Get over it, Nikki.*

✷ ✷ ✷ ✷ ✷

"You are never going to believe this," Nikki spouted loudly when her cousin Roxie answered the overseas call.

"I just finished ogling the most gorgeous excuse for a man that I have ever seen. I just had to call you and fill you in."

"I'm glad you did. I guess you made it there okay?" Roxie asked her.

"Yea, I forgot how long that trip was."

"Well, spill it. Tell me about this man."

Roxie acted like an older sister to Nikki. They behaved more like best friends than cousins. Nikki supported Roxie during her divorce.

She coached Roxie during the labor and delivery of her son, Aaron. Roxie advised Nikki on the decision to leave the states and take the engineering job at the base in England.

"He's a Marine. At least I think he is. He sure looks like one to me. Anyway, he lives next door. I just saw him getting his milk from the front porch. No shirt, I might add. He has the most buffed chest I've ever seen."

"Oh, my! He does sound delicious! But, I thought you were there to get away from men. Now, you've already got your sights on another one?"

"No, not really. I just like to look at him that's all. Trust me, Rox, you'd like to look at him, too," Nikki said a little embarrassed.

"I'm sure I would. But, I thought we made a pact that we were done with the male species for a while?" Roxie asked her.

"I'm not going to go jump his bones or anything, Rox. Well, not today anyway. I'm just sharing the view outside my window with you, that's all," Nikki said rather defensively.

"Well, you keep me posted on the view okay?" Roxie said smiling.

"Don't worry, I will. Tell mom and dad that I made it here all in one piece and that I'll call them later in the week, okay? You are still planning on coming at Christmas, right?"

"I'd like to, but I don't know how I can afford it. John isn't exactly holding up to his side of the divorce agreement," Roxie said disgustedly.

"Look, you're coming. Daddy will pay for it. You have to be here. Don't worry about the money. Okay?"

"Okay," Roxie said exasperated. "I can't wait to see you."

"Me either. Talk to you soon."

* * * * *

Most civilians regarded Menwith Hill Station as a mysterious 'spy' base.

It was common knowledge that Menwith Hill is a communications facility. The falsehoods spread from there as to what and whom the base is actually communicating with. Many locals claim that the US government monitors ALL communications entering and leaving the country, including all personal phone calls, faxes, emails, etc. However, the Americans highly deny this hearsay.

Activists and protesters, or 'the gypsies' as they were fondly referred to because of the small caravans they camped out in, frequently picketed the area across the street from the base. On several occasions, the Ministry of Defense caught people climbing over the fences to the base. Many thrived on gathering as much information about the huge satellite encasing 'golf balls' that collected communications.

Nikki noticed a few cosmetic additions to the Commissary and Base Exchange. Other than that, everything was exactly as she remembered.

Recalling her need for some sundry items, Nikki pulled into the parking lot for the exchange and electronic annex. She rummaged through her purse for the list of things she needed. Once she found it, she popped into the exchange.

Wandering the aisles, Nikki grabbed a few cleaning supplies, snacks and beauty products. As she turned the corner, she saw his broad shoulders towering over the racks of clothing he fumbled through. Nikki hardly recognized him in his green camouflage fatigues.

So he is a Marine puke. Christ, she couldn't have met an easily forgettable army idiot. No, he has to be one of the fucking few and the proud, she thought to herself, recognizing the uniform.

A shiver starting in her toes made her feel like she stood on the edge of the roof of a high building. The tingling made it difficult to appear nonchalant while making her getaway. As if he sensed that someone watched him, he snapped his head up and instantly locked his gaze directly into her eyes and stared at her intently. A smile formed at the corners of his mouth as he slowly walked toward her.

"We meet again, I see," he spoke softly.

"Yeah." She snarled as she juggled the items in her hands dropping a can of squirt cheese and a plastic bottle of body lotion she carried. The cheese rolled across the floor towards Will, bumping up against his boot. He snorted, she thought a little too loudly, and bent down to pick up the can.

"You eat this stuff?"

"I'm all out of bugs and snakes," she said blushing. Nikki hoped that the good Lord would take her right then. Squirt cheese remained one of those nasty little addictions she could not kick and really wanted to keep private. Sometimes late at night it quelled the twinge of hunger and didn't require any great effort. Usually she ate it on crackers, but frequently squirted it directly in her mouth. Her dad often accused her of acting like members of *Animal House*.

"Cheese in a can? That's just not right." He laughed at her again. Nikki snatched the can away from him and turned toward the checkout counter. She did not like this man!

He placed his hand on her arm causing her to turn back in his direction. "What's your name?"

"Is that a request or a demand?" Nikki replied feeling the beginning of anger.

His answer was barely audible. "Just a request, Darlin'."

The tightness immediately returned to her stomach and the whispered response escaped her lips. "My name is Nikki, butthead. And I told you once already I'm not your Darlin'."

"Whoa! What the hell have I done to piss you off?" he asked her as he released his grip on her elbow.

"The fact that you're a man pisses me off, Darlin'." Nikki said finally recovering some of her composure.

Nikki smiled sarcastically at him and headed again for the checkout counter. She glanced back at him nervously. He stood in shock watching her walk out of the door. Nikki could feel the sweat beading on her upper lip. She had never met anyone who flustered her so much. He disconcerted her tremendously. She definitely didn't like him at all! The fact that she was extremely rude and obnoxious to a fellow Marine, and southerner, would be a subject she would not discuss with her father.

* * * * *

Nikki sat in the rented Ford with her head bouncing softly on the steering wheel.

"Damn piece of shit," she said trying to turn the engine over for the fifteenth time.

To make matters worse the British were celebrating another bank holiday this week, therefore, the gas station next door was closed. She was stuck. Her only option involved going next door and asking the gorgeous asshole for help. Chewing nails sounded more appealing than that, but she needed to get to work. Maybe it would prove easily fixable and she could be on her way in a minute. However, she felt by the sound of the engine, this wasn't something easily fixed.

"Shit fire and save the matches," she said as she kicked the front tire with the toe of her black pumps. Wincing, she cursed again as she made her way next door. *This must be God's punishment for acting like such a bitch!*

Will covered his head with his pillow at the sound of the grinding engine. The sound woke him from slumber and continued on for four more screeches. Of course, the day he didn't have to get up early, someone in the neighborhood would have car trouble. He threw his pillow off the bed and stormed over to the window to see who was causing the ruckus.

His first thought was, *Well, fuck her!* However, her voluptuous ass poking out from under the hood was a bit tempting. Why the hell should he help her when she was such a bitch the other day? On that note, he threw himself back into bed and under the covers to go back to sleep.

Her stomach fluttered several times before she could make her finger press the doorbell.

"Oh, good. He's not home," she told herself when Will didn't immediately answer the door. His jeep sat in the driveway so her gut told her he resided in there somewhere. *Maybe he was asleep.* She turned abruptly and began walking down the steps when Will's front door opened.

Will stood there looking absolutely mouthwatering. He rubbed his eyes with one hand and scratched the hairs on his bare chest with the other as he focused on her.

"You're making social calls a bit early this morning don't you think?" He scowled at her.

"This is not a social call," she replied smugly. "My car won't start and the gas station is shut."

"Well, thanks for holding me in such high regard," he said still scowling. "Let me get a shirt on and I'll have a look."

Will left the front door open as he ran upstairs. Nikki couldn't help peeking in and seeing just how the smug jarhead lived. From what she could see, his tastes were surprisingly similar to her own.

"See anything you like?" Will asked her as he bounced down the stairs.

"Just curious," she said blushing. The man seemed to thrive on embarrassing the hell out of her. Nikki turned and headed down the drive toward her car.

After clanking around under the hood of the rental car for what seemed like hours, Will yelled to her to try to turn the engine over again. Nikki shook her head trying to release her eyes from his backside, which she fixated on during his exploration of the problem.

Turning the key slowly, Nikki cringed when the grinding of metal shrieked again from the engine.

"Well, Darlin'," he said just to annoy her. "I'm afraid you're shit out of luck. This thing has seen better days."

"Damn it! How the hell am I going to get to work?"

"Maybe if you asked nicely, I could take you in," Will said, batting his luscious eyelashes at her.

"I really didn't want to bother you, but I had no choice," Nikki said avoiding his gaze.

"That's okay. I was only sleeping. Why don't you just lighten up a bit, Darlin'? I'd be happy to take you to work."

"Okay. If you really wouldn't mind, I would really appreciate it."

Her palms perspired profusely on the way to the base. She hoped he didn't notice her nervousness. He invariably seemed relaxed and poised around her. It must be the Marine in him.

Damn. Will hoped she didn't notice his *woody* coming to attention. If her skirt inched up any further on those creamy thighs of hers, he was going to spew!

Nikki began to open the car door before he came to a complete stop at her office.

"Thanks again. I really appreciate it," she said without looking him in the eye.

"I can pick you up later if you need a ride home."

"No thanks. I'll call the rental place and have them bring me another car."

"Well, you know where I am if you're ever needing a butthead," Will said winking at her as he drove away.

Scowling, Nikki stormed into her office and threw her briefcase on her desk. That man absolutely unnerved her! It would be a cold day in hell before she asked him for anything again!

Nikki picked up her office phone and waited for the long distance operator.

"Roxie, you have got to hear this," Nikki said. "I have never met anyone as arrogant and obnoxious as that Marine guy!"

"What on earth happened?"

"Well, my freaking car wouldn't start so I had to ask him to look at it. Of course, it still wouldn't start so he brought me to work. He was so smug I just wanted to slap him! I wish I didn't ever have to lay eyes on his obnoxious ass again!"

"I hate to break this to you, but you're going to have to," Roxie said cautiously.

"What are you talking about?" Nikki asked her irritatingly.

"Because you have to show him some form of southern hospitality for helping you out. What would your daddy say if you didn't show him some form of thank you?" Roxie asked her.

"Oh shit, Roxie. Why do you always have to be so perfect?"

✳ ✳ ✳ ✳ ✳

The weekend brought a third day in a row of sunshine and warm weather. People literally collapsed on the street during the seventy-two degree "heat wave" that swept over the area.

Nikki lay on the lawn chair in her backyard wearing a skimpy bikini. Why she felt it necessary to bring it in the first place was questionable, but she delighted in the fact she did. She didn't care that goose pimples from the cool breeze blowing, covered her entire body. The sun shone brightly, and she intended to soak it in. She sipped on a diet soda and enjoyed a historical romance. Will stood in the window of his bedroom upstairs awed at the sight of her creamy skin against the neon green two-piece swimsuit, if you could call it that much. He sat quietly on his bed just staring at her. What a day this turned out to be. He thought he recognized her stiff, protruding nipples as a symptom of the temperature she was combating. If those things poked out any further they'd bust loose. Will stayed there for thirty-three minutes. She reached her limit. He watched her while she began packing up her things to go back in the house.

Bent over, to fold up the lawn chair, Nikki's bikini bottoms rode up snugly between her firm buttocks. Will snickered as she removed the inconvenience and shook her bottom slightly on the way into the house. *Well, fuck me!* She would die if she knew what he saw her just do. Will didn't know what to do about that neighbor of his, but as God was his witness, it would be something, and sometime soon.

Chapter Four

Nikki waited anxiously for her first check before darkening the doors of the quaint little shops in which she dearly loved to squander her time and money. Finally, payday arrived so she decided to pop into the *Joiner* and grab a drink, to celebrate.

"Hello, Tex!" said Ian.

"Hi, Ian."

"You look exceptionally brilliant this afternoon."

"Thank you. I feel exceptionally brilliant today, I got my first real paycheck," she said with her eyes glistening.

"Success suits you."

"I plan on it suiting me for a long time," she said smiling smugly. "How about a pint, Sir Bartender?"

"I still can't understand why a lovely, feminine lady like you would order such a manly size beverage. Ladies order a half-pint."

"I'm from Texas, Ian. We like things big," she said a bit seductively.

He raised an eyebrow and smiled at her remark. "Aren't you the cheeky one?"

She finished her drink and continued her conversation with Ian. The subject bounced from Nikki trying to adjust to her new life, to Ian's problem with food and drink suppliers. Ian possessed a flair for conversation, an international standard for proper innkeepers, and Nikki genuinely enjoyed his company.

Ian Canterbury masqueraded as the typical local pub owner one would see on British television. He had introduced Nikki to his wife, Victoria, a few nights ago when she came to visit him in the pub.

It comforted Nikki to see two people love each other so completely. She remembered her parents being the same way even after twenty-five years of marriage. David and Allison often passed looks, holding complete conversations without speaking a single word. Although she'd never admit it to anyone, Nikki yearned for that kind of true love. Both couples were examples of the kind of relationship she wanted.

Thoughts of Will Chambers crossed her mind continuously. Shaking her head, Nikki unsuccessfully tried to remove the ridiculous thought of him as her lover.

Brandon had found sex more entertaining than she did. Nikki didn't understand what all the fuss was about. She let Brandon get his fill of her because she thought she loved him. You gave it up to the man you loved, even if you didn't want to.

Looking back, she wished she saved herself for that one true love. Oh, well, you can't go back. The next man she decided to take on damned well better see she enjoyed it. Otherwise, she might as well join a convent.

There must be more to sex than the experiences she endured with Brandon. One thing for certain, she damn sure wouldn't tolerate any man breaking her spirit again. *This is it. Nikki Phillips, take me as I am or fuck you!*

Nikki left the pub and drove home. As she entered the gate to her house, she glanced next door and noticed Will's jeep in his driveway. Her heart seemed to add an additional beat at the thought of him. She used all her considerable abilities to force visions of his sexy ass bending over the hood of her piece of shit, rental car out of her mind. It wasn't working.

* * * * *

The First Armored Division pulled back into Kuwait City. The screams of women and children echoed through Will's head as he slowly trudged along. A small boy of about seven clung desperately to Will's leg begging for food. Will looked into his eyes; his face dirty and streaked with tears. Will threw down a MRE. The boy slumped over the ration, gathering it up quickly before anyone else saw him. Will watched him as he hid it in his clothes and ran back to his mother.

The stench of death hung in the air as the division continued on through the chaos. Fires burned all around them charring the mutilated bodies that were too unrecognizable to bury. A soldier's uniform lay in the road in front of them. Will bent down to pick it up only to discover that it was still occupied. Waves of nausea pierced through him as he heaved and tried to swallow the bile coming up in his throat –

The sheets lay twisted around him, saturated with his sweat. Would he ever be able to shake these horrible memories? Will laid back on the pillows allowing his breathing to return to its normal rhythm. Finally, he peeled his wet skin from the sheets to go downstairs to the kitchen.

Will passed by the window in his living room and saw Nikki's long legs dangling out of the car. Although in desperate need of sleep, he remained there watching her.

He was screwed! Will found himself watching Nikki in an attempt to soothe himself back from the horror of nightmares robbing him of his sanity. There she stood, just outside his window, in all her glory. Why couldn't he stop thinking about her? It's not like she was losing any sleep over him. He either woke up in a sweating mass of hysteria or with a major hard-on. *What the hell was the matter with him?*

Will admired the way Nikki carried herself in business attire. She looked flawless to him in her black suit that clung to her every curve. Her legs, complimented by silky black stockings and black pumps, took long strides up the steps. He peeked at her through his window while she fumbled for her keys. Nikki dropped them on the stairs and as she bent down to pick them up, Will felt a tingle through his loins. She collected the keys and unlocked her door. He turned from the window as she walked inside. *Oh, what the hell!*

Nikki put her purse down by the telephone table and went upstairs to change clothes. She grabbed her favorite flannel pants, white t-shirt and then pulled on some thick, warm socks to go downstairs and make some tea. After putting the kettle on, she went into the living room to watch some TV until the whistle blew.

The fire she built warmed and relaxed her. Nikki adored the way the heat from it thawed her toes as she stretched out on the sofa. The kettle called to her, breaking the bubble of her relaxation.

Nikki sliced a lemon and placed it on the tea tray along with the teapot, her favorite cup, and some artificial sweetener. She walked back into the living room and set the tray on the table in front of the fireplace. Fixing the tea to her liking, she sat back to unwind. The tea soothed her as it rolled down the back of her throat. Smiling, she remembered her dad referring to hot tea as British antifreeze.

At the loud chiming of the doorbell, she startled and spilled the hot tea on her pants.

"Damn it!" she exclaimed as she jumped off the sofa. "Who in the hell—?" Her words trailed off as she went down the hallway to answer the door.

He mimicked a marionette as if someone stood above him pulling the strings, manipulating him to put his clothes on, as he walked to her house. He needed to feel her presence close to him. *He was fucked!* That's the only phrase to describe how he felt. He was determined to make Nikki his. He just quite hadn't figured out how…yet.

"Don't you look adorable?" Will said in his slow southern drawl when Nikki opened the door.

"You're easily impressed," she said with a sheepish smile.

"You want to come in?" Her voice perturbed her when it shook as she spoke to him.

"I was hoping you'd ask."

"Would you like some tea? I was just wearing some myself when the doorbell rang," she said rolling her eyes as she pulled at the front of her pants.

She tried desperately to muster up all the southern hospitality that was possible since her rotten cousin reminded her it was the proper thing to do. She basically was a nice person. However, she didn't want any man to take it as a reason to steamroll her.

"I don't drink that fancy hot stuff."

"I have some iced tea in the fridge." Nikki forced a smile at him as she went into the kitchen.

"You're all right, you know it?" He said as he placed his hand on her shoulder.

"You might think I wasn't a real Texan, if I didn't have iced tea. Actually, I always keep some in the fridge just in case some lost southerner drops by for directions." She handed him his glass and they turned to go in the living room.

Nikki sat down on the sofa and fixed herself another cup. Will sat down in the chair across from her and watched her intently as she sipped carefully.

"Got any plans tomorrow?" he asked, cautiously observing her face.

"Why do you ask?" she asked trying to avoid his eyes. Will invariably seemed to be looking directly into her when he spoke. It made her uncomfortable. His gaze caught her off guard.

"Somehow I sense that question was asked in order to discuss the subject of your plans for tomorrow," Nikki continued.

Nikki's quick wit and ability to fathom what seemed an obvious ploy on his part amused him, "Would you like some plans?"

"Okay, I'll bite. What did you have in mind?"

"That's classified. If I told you, I'd have to kill you."

"Charming," she said as she rubbed her sweaty palms on her pants.

"I'll pick you up around ten. Okay?"

"Okay," she said trying desperately to think of something clever to say. Her mind froze. Nikki couldn't quite explain why she agreed, but she did. Before she knew it, the word had escaped her.

Will looked her straight in the eye, winked at her, drained his iced tea and rose from the chair. Without further comment, he made his way back to the front door and let himself out.

His wink left her stuck to her seat and added with yet another beat of her heart to punctuate the moment. Nikki glanced disgustedly in the hallway mirror. *What in the hell just happened? I just had to listen to Roxie.*

Will smirked to himself all the way back home. He knew that she only agreed to go with him because she felt she owed it to him for helping her out the other day. However, he was going to play this for all it was worth. He wondered how long it took to chip away at an Ice Queen. He'd sure have fun finding out.

Chapter Five

At 9:35 a.m. her doorbell rang.

"Shit!" She poked her eye with the mascara brush when the chime, just outside the bathroom door, startled her. She went downstairs in her sleeping clothes and pulled the door open leaving her gazing into Will's deep blue eyes.

Her eyes traveled down the dark hairs flirting out the top of the blue t-shirt he wore tucked into faded jeans. On his feet were his boots. She knew he must wear them with everything but his uniform, considering their scuffed appearance. Her heart fluttered in her chest as she stepped back in surprise.

God, she was beautiful! Will loved the way she looked with her silky black hair pulled up in a hurried ponytail. She wore an oversized pink sweatshirt hanging off one shoulder. Will observed no unsightly bra strap. Her erect nipples teased him through the fabric. The tight black leggings she wore accentuated her long curvy legs.

Will brought his hand to the side of his mouth to avoid an embarrassing show of drool escaping. He prayed she didn't notice his arousal beginning between his legs.

"You're early," she said sounding a little irritated.

"The sun's out," he stated flatly, "God knows that's a rare enough occurrence around here. We can't waste a day with good sunshine now can we, Darlin'? You never know when we're going to have another one."

Will pushed the door open wider and walked across the threshold. Those blue eyes pierced through her like lasers. When he smiled at her, the lines around those beautiful eyes got deeper. Nikki wanted to touch his face and trace all of his laugh lines with her fingers...*or tongue*, at this moment it made no difference. He smelled fresh of soap and aftershave. His scent drew her in to him and made her chest tingle. *Damnation!*

"I'm not even dressed, yet."

"Then run up and get dressed," he said as his eyes mapped the length of her body. "I'll fix us a cup of coffee. You do have coffee don't you?"

"Of course," she said with a touch of ice in her voice. "You still never told me where we are going."

Nikki turned around to head upstairs. Will stared at the lovely way her tight pants flattered her shape. He wanted to get his hands on her ass so badly he clenched his fists, to fight off the urge.

"I like cream in my coffee," she yelled down from her bedroom.

"I'll give you cream," he whispered.

Nikki pulled on a pair of faded jeans that slid easily over her hips. Admiring her backside in the mirror, she tucked in a white t-shirt and then pulled on a baggy red sweater. Opting for the red roper boots, over the other two pairs in her closet, she quickly pulled them on her feet. She couldn't leave Texas without them.

She brushed her hair and pulled it up in a fresh ponytail. Dabbing her favorite perfume between her breasts, she stood to finish her makeup in the mirror.

"Coffee's ready," Will called from the kitchen.

He watched her long legs make their way down the stairs. He felt his chest tighten as he took her all in. As he handed her a cup, their fingers brushed together gently. She brought the cup to her red, luscious lips and sipped quietly. Will desperately wanted to take those lips with his and taste the coffee on her tongue.

"Love the boots," he said smiling slyly when his eyes got to her feet.

"I thought you might." She couldn't believe she said that.

Maybe he wouldn't notice her hands trembling.

No man made her this nervous. Something about this man did though, and it sure pissed her off.

They sat at the dining table and drank their coffee. Her scent drifted across the table to him. The sweetness of it made chills run down his back. He could get lost in those gorgeous blue-green eyes.

"So, what made you ask me out today?" Nikki asked him breaking the awkward silence.

"Ever since I saw you in the pub, I couldn't stop thinking about you," he said flatly and winking at her.

Could he see her heart pounding in her chest?

"Don't you have a girl in every port...so the saying goes?"

"Not this cowboy. Besides, that's the Navy, not the Marines. And, I personally have never met a squid that was up to the rumor."

She smiled at the slang reference to sailors that her father used so many times.

"I'll be here for a couple of years. We could have a lot of fun in that time, don't you think?" he asked her smiling devilishly.

Nikki swallowed hard, dislodging her heart from her throat. She chose not to reply to his question.

"I didn't think Marines were supposed to show emotions."

Will raised an eyebrow up at her. "That's just a factual statement, Darlin', not an emotion. How do you know so much about Marines anyway?"

"I'm a Marine brat. My father used to be the commanding officer of your detachment. I've been here before. My mom is from here." She was flustered by her diarrhea of the mouth.

"Semper Fi," he said simply.

"Right back at ya."

He drank down the last swallow of the now cool coffee. "So, are you ready to head out?" he asked her.

"As ready as I'll ever be." Nikki replied.

As they walked out the front door, Will softly placed his hand along her back. The heat from his touch rose up the back of her neck causing her to shiver.

Will could tell he made her nervous, and he liked it. She acted tough, but he knew that she could easily be putty in his hands.

The sweater she wore accentuated her breasts. He wondered if she ever wore a bra. Crossing her arms in front of her she attempted to camouflage her nipples stiffening under her clothes. Too late, Will already noticed.

He tracked up her long neckline to her pouty mouth, imagining how soft and smooth her skin appeared. Will wanted to cup her breasts and kiss them until she couldn't breathe. *Patience was a virtue, wasn't it?* No man could rush a woman like her.

The thought of courting her amused him. He wanted to woo her. He'd never believed in love at first sight but something about her mesmerized him.

Will waited his whole life to experience feelings like this for someone. Sure, he dated plenty of women, but they always lacked something. He never felt the connection and the chemistry that she provided. He anticipated the chase to capture her.

She could take him right now, she thought to herself. Why did he always stare at her? His muscles rippled against his T-shirt. Those dark, curly hairs that peeked out the top of every shirt the man owned teased her to come and play with them. Remembering how he looked a few mornings ago on his front porch shot chills through to her core.

She'd never felt sensations through her body like the ones he sent through her. All it took was one look into his eyes, one touch of his hands, one breath on her skin and she tingled. Nikki envisioned caressing him, feeling his tight buttocks as he moved in her. God, what was she thinking? This was going too fast. Why did she keep having visions of screwing him? She struggled with herself not to get carried away by his charms.

Being the daughter of a US Marine made a person respect their values and honor. Nikki remembered her father in his dress blues and how handsome he looked. She envisioned how scrumptious Will would look in his. She wondered if she'd ever see him in that uniform.

They drove through the countryside to the coast and eventually parked near the beach. Will got out and opened the back of his jeep, removing a picnic basket and blanket. It amused her the way he obviously planned ahead for this little excursion. Exactly what did he think this little payback would get him? He grabbed her hand and led her down close to the water. The cold air made her feel alive and refreshed.

Will neatly placed the blanket on the ground and opened up the picnic basket. He removed cheese, crackers, strawberries and two splits of champagne. He took out two champagne flutes and filled them with the sparkling beverage. Nikki took the glass he offered her and sipped delicately. She adored the way it felt down the back of her throat. He arranged food on both plates and handed one to Nikki.

They ate quietly. Periodically, he questioned her about her life. Nikki's lips were feeling slightly numb. Glancing at the empty champagne bottle, she could not remember him refilling her glass. But he must have—and more than once. He smiled at her in his bewitching manner when he realized she was on to him. Curiosity filled her thoughts. He just thought he could handle her? Was she willing to prove him wrong?

Except for the necessary trysts that helped him keep his sanity, Will actively avoided women. He didn't know if there would ever be a woman that he could share his secrets with. That would make him vulnerable and that was not a trait he desired to have.

Something about her called to him when she walked into the pub that first time. He wasn't sure why he was drawn to her. It certainly wasn't her bursting personality and her easy way with men. He was determined to break the shell she hid inside of and find out what made her tick.

They pulled into his driveway. He placed his hand on the back of her neck as they walked over to her front door. His fingers amazed her, leaving heat on her skin, even through her clothes. She refused to turn around and get caught up in his eyes.

He gently lifted her hand to his lips and brushed a kiss across her knuckles.

"Thanks for a wonderful day," she said avoiding his gaze.

"There are lots more where that one came from."

Nikki stood in the doorway and watched him as he walked next door and up onto his porch. Turning, he winked at her and then closed the door. Nikki made her way upstairs to her bedroom attempting half-heartedly to forget about the man who made her feel like chivalry really wasn't dead.

Chapter Six

Nikki couldn't prevent thoughts of Will from infiltrating her head. Her work kept her busy, but she caught herself during the day having glimpses of him pop into her mind. *Was he thinking about her, too?* Keeping her nose to the grindstone, Nikki attempted to keep from sitting at home thinking about him.

The fact remained the man was everywhere. Nikki saw him with his buddies at the club during lunch. Little did she know he couldn't keep his eyes off of her when he spotted her laughing with her co-workers. Although, she attempted to avoid him, Nikki found herself bumping into him all over the base.

Her presence unnerved him. His stomach tightened whenever he spotted her anywhere on the base. Will couldn't stop staring at her. He loved the way her laughter caught him unaware across a crowded room. *That could be because he never heard it when she was with him…unless; some Marine was being tortured on the base. He could see her getting a real kick out of that.* He couldn't stand it anymore. He needed to see her again and soon. Today.

✷ ✷ ✷ ✷ ✷

Nikki awaited payday anxiously so she could buy a car. She'd driven that piece-of-shit rental car for as long as she could stand.

After changing into comfortable clothes, she jogged down the stairs just as the doorbell rang. Will stood on the bottom step with his cap under his arm. He looked dreadfully tired. It flattered her he came to her before going home to relax or change clothes.

"How are you?" he asked her stepping inside.

"Great! Today was payday. I actually think I am going to be able to eat this month! You look like hammered dog shit." She turned to walk down the hallway toward the den.

"Gee, you really know how to make a guy feel good about himself. Does that come natural for you, or what? I'd hate for you to starve and let that squishy butt of yours get too bony." He raised an eyebrow as he looked to her for a reaction.

"Excuse me? My butt is not squishy!" she scowled at him thinking of how many squats she had completed the day before in an attempt to tighten her gluts.

"Well, maybe squishy isn't the right word. Voluptuous is more suitable, I think."

"I don't think I want to talk to you about the consistency of my ass if you don't mind." She punched him a bit harder than he expected in the arm.

"I like your ass. I meant it only as a compliment, Darlin', I swear."

"And when have you been looking at my ass, may I ask?"

"Pretty much anytime I've seen you. It looked pretty damned tasty the other day when you bent down to pick up your keys," he stated firmly before realizing he had said it out loud.

"You were watching me?"

"Uh, yeah...by accident...I was walking past my front window when you came home and I just happened to glance over toward your house just in the nick of time."

"Yeah, sure." She turned to glare at him.

He grabbed her face in his hands and looked into her eyes. "I can't help myself with you, Darlin'. You are the most beautiful thing I have ever seen. I've wanted to do this since the first time I saw you."

He took her mouth, quickly, before she could stop him. The heat rose up her throat as she felt his tongue exploring the depths of her mouth. She dove into him uncontrollably until she could feel the sweat on the back of her neck. He nibbled her lips and then traveled down her neck with his tongue.

She threw her head back in delight as he continued down the front of her shirt. Holding his head in her hands, and leading him back up to her mouth, she kissed him, this time with all the fervor that filled her. Nikki sensed the tingle in her breasts, as her nipples hardened. She pulled away abruptly and stared at him.

"Whoa," she whispered.

"I'll say," he replied.

He couldn't remember feeling this kind of burning desire for any woman. He wanted to rip her clothes off and kiss every inch of her. He wanted to feel her hot tongue in his mouth and over his body. *With all the fire that she lashed him with, over the last few days, he assumed she would taste of burning cayenne pepper. Amazingly, she tasted sugary sweet. What am I getting myself into?*

"Is it hot in here?" she asked him shyly, as she fanned the top of her shirt.

"I think you are the one who got the temperature up in here. I never knew anyone could be sexy in flannel."

"Oh, trust me. They can," she said remembering again that morning he stood on his front porch.

"You got any food in there? Suddenly, I could eat a…a…horse. I'll even help you whip something up," Will told her trying to force the heat down that welled up in his chest.

"Only if you swear not to pull that kind of stunt again. Next time, I'll have to take you down," she said slapping him upside the head.

Yea, I'd like you to take me down. "I like it when a woman takes the initiative."

Nikki rolled her eyes at him and stalked towards the kitchen.

They rummaged through the refrigerator and the kitchen cabinets, finally opting for a quick pasta dish. Will cut the vegetables, while Nikki marinated the chicken. She pulled out a bottle of wine and poured each of them a glass. She was surprised at the comfort she felt having a man who felt at home in her kitchen. She put the pasta on to boil and went into the dining room to set the table.

Nikki decided on the good china located in the buffet. She came across some candles in the drawer, lit them, and placed them in the center of the table. By the time she returned to the kitchen, Will held plates in hand steaming with food. She grabbed their wine glasses and preceded him to the dining room.

"My, my, are you trying to seduce me with a romantic dinner?" he asked her, as he looked at the table.

"Hardly. I eat like this all the time; even when I'm by myself. Presentation is everything," she said as she brushed her hand over the top of his head. They ate their meal slowly, doing more talking than eating. Conversation became easier between them. The candles burned down to the candlestick by the time they finished. When Nikki blew them out, gently, Will's stomach tightened as he watched her mouth.

Her lips, wet with wine, beckoned his. He leaned over the table attempting to kiss her.

"You really don't want to go there," she said, not too convincingly.

"I couldn't control myself," he flirtatiously said.

"I thought Marines prided themselves on control?"

"Uh...yea...I guess I failed that part in boot camp."

"I'll say." Nikki picked up their plates and headed toward the kitchen. Will followed her with the rest of the dishes. They finished cleaning up, and returned to the living room.

"What are you doing tomorrow?" Will asked her.

"I'm going to buy me a car."

"I love to buy cars. I'll be here around 9:30."

"But—" she stood with her mouth agape.

"I guess I should be heading on out then," he said, as he quickly let himself out. He couldn't believe he was cutting the evening short but he knew that he needed to take things slow. If he stayed any longer he would have to ravish her.

"But—"

She stood staring at the open door.

"Where did I lose control of this conversation?" She said aloud, pressing her head to the back of the door.

✱ ✱ ✱ ✱ ✱

"This is getting really scary, Rox," Nikki said when her cousin answered the phone.

"What on earth? Do you know what time it is?" Roxie asked yawning.

"Yes, it's 10:00 here, so that means...uh, oh, sorry Roxie. I guess it's four in the morning there, huh?"

"Yea, this better be good and you better not have woke up Aaron, or I'm going to really kill you next time I see you. So, what's so scary?"

"Remember the view, from my window, I told you about?"

"Yea, the gorgeous hunk in flannel?"

"Yea, well, he just kissed me. And we sort of have a date tomorrow."

"No shit? You're working pretty fast, for someone who didn't want a man in her life."

"Tell me about it. God, Roxie, I think I'm in real trouble." Nikki said, a bit sadly.

"So, tell me about this kiss. John kissed like a fish, so I have to live vicariously through you."

"It made my knees buckle and I really thought I was going to pass out."

"Oh, God, you've got it bad, girl. Was there any tongue?"

"Yea, a little, but it was the sexiest little bit of tongue I have ever had. I swear I thought I was going to cream my pants!"

"Shit, Nikki, you're dead!" Roxie said, laughing hysterically. "I can't believe you haven't even been there a month yet, and already you've found the man of your dreams. What am I going to do with you?"

"Help me! Shit, Roxie, I didn't want this. But, I didn't exactly say he was the man of my dreams."

"Not in so many words, no, but what did your momma always tell you...*Actions speak louder than words*," Roxie said facetiously. "It sounds to me like he has it pretty bad for you, too."

"You think? This scares the hell out of me, Rox."

"I know, but all I can say is, follow your heart."

"That's what I was afraid of."

Chapter Seven

Nikki awoke early the next morning. Her body tingled from the incredible dream she experienced, Will kissing every inch of her. As she lay on her back remembering her dream, she noticed her nipples protruding against the cotton of her shirt. They ached at the thought of him holding them firmly in his strong hands.

The need overcame her to touch, to feel, and to explore the sensations of her own body. With Brandon, sex meant less than nothing. He thrilled in getting his rocks off. Nikki realized, better late than never, if she wouldn't give it to him, he would get it from someone else. In fact, he'd done just that, many times.

It amazed Nikki how a man could make her feel this sexual with just one kiss. Okay, maybe more than just one. God, how the heat surged through her veins when his lips met hers. *I think I'm in big trouble,* she said to herself.

Closing her eyes, Nikki slowly slid her hand down to the slickness that thoughts of Will created between her legs. As she gently rubbed the sensitive nub, it hardened with desire. Nikki moaned deeply in her throat, as she envisioned Will kissing her there.

She pulled the hard nipple on her breast, as she continued to satisfy her own desires. Feeling the rush of orgasm through her fingers, for the first time she experienced a wave of release, rush through her body. Nikki lay there quietly for a few moments as her body relaxed. *Damn,* she said. *I've never done THAT before.*

Nikki stood on her shaky legs and headed toward the bathroom. She filled the claw-footed tub with hot bubbly water and slid in, to bathe. Her choice of citrus scented bath soap refreshed and revitalized her. As she soaked in the warm bubbles, picturing Will in her mind, she questioned if he could possibly be any more handsome than he appeared last night. His irresistibility increased each time she saw him.

Nikki spent thirty minutes trying to figure out what to wear. *Why does he make me so nervous?* She finally settled on a pair of comfortable jeans, a tight, knit, scalloped neck sweater, to show just enough cleavage, and her boots, of course. Pulling her hair up in a clip, she let tendrils hang down the back of her neck. A small amount of makeup and perfume dabbed in strategic places finished her off, so she headed downstairs.

As the coffee brewed, she transferred the items from her big purse into a small shoulder bag. The small one could go across her body, freeing her hands to rip his heart out, if necessary. She sipped her coffee, and ate half a bagel while she waited for Will to come over.

Hunger escaped her. Her stomach contained no room for food due to the massive number of butterflies that fluttered within. She toyed with the idea of leaving the house before he arrived, to avoid him altogether.

Will flew out of bed when he glanced up at the clock and it read 9:00. He couldn't seem to wake himself up when the alarm went off. He extensively enjoyed his dream of Nikki. It began where they left off last night and ended with her waking him with her fingers, massaging his shaft. The shock of waking up late made his erection flaccid again.

He took a quick shower, shaved and got dressed. He tucked in a long sleeved, cranberry colored, baby corduroy shirt into his favorite jeans. He then pulled on his boots. His clock read 9:25.

Will left no time for coffee. He expected Nikki would have some brewing. Some women mattered too much to keep waiting. Will grabbed his leather jacket and walked over to Nikki's. His palms perspired more than normal as he depressed the doorbell.

Nikki radiated beauty when she answered the door. It amazed Will how the slightest hint of makeup accentuated her most exquisite features.

"You look great, Nikki."

"Thanks. Would you like some coffee?" Obviously, the morning suited him, too. But, she'd be damned if she'd tell him that.

"I knew I *loved* you for some reason. You must have read my mind." *That should really piss her off.* He thought to himself. *I can already see the steam coming out of her ears.*

Nikki startled at his statement. *Did he really say what I think he said?* "I have to have my morning kick in the pants, or I'm no good to anyone."

Nikki fixed him a cup then picked hers up, and sipped it carefully. She showed him the automobile ads in the newspaper of the ones that interested her.

"Kind of flashy, don't you think?" he asked her, as he smiled into his cup.

"I've always wanted something like this." She showed him the bright red convertible on the page. "My parents were always so conservative. I got the family car after they got sick of it. It's my money, so I'm going to buy what I want."

"Well, come on, Spunky. Let's get moving."

She laughed at his nickname for her, as she grabbed her jacket. He placed his hand on the back of her neck as they walked next door, to get into his jeep.

"What? No picnic basket?" she asked him jokingly.

"Not this time. I thought we could grab a bite in town. Besides, you're going to owe me lunch when I get you a good deal on the car you want."

"Exactly how many times do I have to be Miss Manners and pay you back for stuff?"

They went into the car dealership and there sat *the* car, on the showroom floor, although not in Nikki's color. Her body melted in the luxurious leather seats. Will slid into the seat next to her. Her eyes glistened, as she ran her petite hands over the steering wheel.

They took it out for a test drive and, after much haggling, came to a deal. The dealership agreed to special order the convertible in Hot Candy Apple Red. She could pick it up in a week. Nikki's thrill electrified her so much that her guard was thrown down. Before she realized her reaction, she flung her arms around Will's neck and kissed him thoroughly.

"Holy shit," she said as she pulled herself away.

"Oh, no. Thank you. I'll have to go shopping with you more often. I've got some ocean front property I could make you a deal on, too." He smiled at her tenderly as they walked out of the dealership.

They found a cozy little Italian restaurant on the outskirts of town. They sat at the back in a small booth. She looked up from her menu to catch a glimpse of him, but caught him already admiring her. The gooseflesh began to rise up her arms when he winked at her. Shifting in her seat, her knee rubbed against his. Will very gently placed his hand on her thigh. She placed her hand on top of his thigh.

Leaning over she whispered in his ear, "I can still hurt you at any time."

Her whisper in his ear made his body pulsate with arousal.

"Here's to your first car, Spunky," he said to her.

"I'll drink to that." He turned to face her, placed his hand under her chin and brought her into him. His mouth covered hers completely. He very gently pulled away, and kissed her lovingly on each corner of her mouth, and then on the tip of her nose. She shuddered as she opened her eyes to see him gazing into them.

"You have the most beautiful eyes I've ever seen," he told her. "They mesmerize me."

She blushed and glanced away to see the waitress coming with their entrees.

They started in on their meals, temporarily easing the sexual tension between them. Will refilled her wine glass, for the second time. The bottle was nearly empty. She could feel her head beginning to spin. She couldn't decide if her nervousness, or the ample amount of wine consumed had created the feeling.

Having a weakness for chocolate, Nikki very rarely indulged herself with dessert, but she thought she deserved it today.

"Please bring me a large piece of the 'Death by Chocolate' Cake. And two forks," she winked at Will. "I can't ever finish the whole thing."

"And two coffees," Will chimed in.

Will put his arm around her waist and pulled her closer to him. Nikki wriggled uncomfortably. "Why do I make you so nervous?" he asked her.

"I honestly don't know. But, I don't like it!"

"You don't like me touching you?"

"I don't like the fact that I can't seem to resist you."

"Who said you need to resist me?"

"Me."

Just then, the waitress returned with their dessert and coffees. Nikki poured cream in hers, and stirred it gently. Will took his fork and took a healthy bite of the cake.

"You were right. You could die from this," he said, motioning to the cake.

Nikki took a bite and closed her eyes in appreciation.

"Oooh, this is wonderful."

"You're pretty wonderful." Will told her as he turned her face towards him.

This woman grabbed his heart so hard, and so fast, it made his head spin. Nikki Phillips was funny, abrupt, sassy, and too damned smart for her own good. All this rolled up into one absolutely mouth watering package.

"How can you say that? You hardly know me. Men will say anything to get in a girl's pants. I'm not that easy."

"Easy is not the word I would ever use to describe you, Darlin'. Someone must've broken your heart pretty good for you to be so down on men in general." Desperately wanting her to open up to him completely, he fixed his gaze on her eyes.

"I never said someone broke my heart. I said no one would ever use me again. There's a big difference."

"There's no difference, Nikki. You can't be used if they don't capture your heart."

He squeezed her hand and looked deep into her eyes. "All you can do is trust in me. I've never been attracted to anyone I just met. To be honest, I can't explain these feelings in me. All I know is that I want to be with you. Why, I don't know. But, the fact that you're drop dead gorgeous might have something to do with it!" *Shit, she's gonna blow again*, he said to himself, when he saw the fire return to her eyes.

"Is that all I am to you, an attraction?" Nikki turned away from him quickly, the swell of anger taking over her body.

"You know that's not what I meant."

Will had gone out with a few women from the base. Lately, his new routine consisted of two hours at the gym, before coming back to an empty house.

"Women were the last thing on my mind, until I saw you."

"I might enjoy being with you, sometimes. That's what scares me. I can't say that I have ever felt this way about anyone before, either. What do we do now?" she said furrowing her brow.

"First, finish our dessert. Then, you can let me kiss you again."

Nikki took another bite of chocolate. Will smiled when he noticed the frosting in the corner of her mouth. He raised his hand to her mouth and wiped off the chocolate with his thumb. He then put his thumb to his mouth and tasted the chocolate on his tongue.

"What in the hell do you think you're doing?" she asked him jokingly.

"Trying to get a rise out of you. Did it work?" He slid his fingers up and down her arm.

"Everything about you gets a rise out of me and I think you know it!"

"How about we blow this joint?" Will said to her, as he kissed her briefly on the top of her head. He tensed up waiting for the blow he knew she'd throw at him. However, seconds later he was still standing. *Hmmm, she didn't disembowel me, so maybe she's lightening up.*

"It's going to be okay, Nikki. I promise."

Would it kill her to have a little bit of fun? It's not like he's not gorgeous, and a very good kisser. Besides, all work and no play makes Jack wank off. Didn't she just do that, too? Maybe a good fuck is what she needed anyway. She just bet his dick was huge!

✱ ✱ ✱ ✱ ✱

A week later Nikki traded the rental car for her new convertible. The cool wind whipped through her hair, causing men to do double takes, as she sped by them.

She drove on the base to register her new car with the officials in the gatehouse. The guys behind the desk had a few provocative words to say to her. *Maybe it's just the car.* She laughed at herself as she got back in the vehicle.

Nikki dropped into the commissary to grab a few items. She attempted to locate American products only available on the base. Craving something spicy, she found the ingredients needed for a good ol' Tex-Mex meal, except for the avocados that resembled rocks in appearance and texture. Nikki decided they were unsuitable to make the guacamole she craved. She hadn't planned on having company, but her subconscious told her to buy enough for two.

Nikki loaded her bags in the car and stopped by the liquor store to pick up a bottle of zinfandel. Nikki pulled into the post office, and spied Will's jeep parked by the entrance. Pretending to be looking for something in her purse, she tried to swallow the lump in her throat. When Will emerged, he spotted her immediately. In fact, everyone noticed her. That car made it impossible not to. A smirk formed on his lips as he walked over to her slowly.

Determined not to look desperate, he spent more time at the gym than usual curbing his desire to show up at her doorstep. He paced himself. At least that's what he kept telling his conscience. Women didn't like men who followed them around like puppies. Not any woman he cared to have anything to do with. *Shit, what Marine acted like that anyway?*

"Hey, Spunky."

"Oh, Hi," she said, acting surprised to see him.

"The car looks great."

"Thanks. I really love it."

"So, what are you up to?" Will asked, rubbing his fingers across her cheek.

"I had to run a few errands. If you're off tonight we could have an 'I got my new car' celebration."

"Are you asking me out?" He said smiling seductively at her.

"I was in the mood to cook. I seemed to have bought enough for an army...uh, I mean a Corps... and I thought you might like to come over. If you have something else to do, go do it. It's no skin off my back," she shot back at him.

"I didn't mean it that way. I just can't believe you're actually inviting me over. I'd love to come as long as I'm not on the menu. I have not had any good southern cooking since I got here."

"You make me sound like a real bitch. I am just trying to be nice," she told him, as she twirled her hair in her fingers.

"That's even better. I like nice. I do nice. What time?"

"Okay, okay. How about six?"

"I'll see you then."

Before she could stop him, he grabbed the back of her neck and planted a hard smacking kiss across her mouth. Her lips stung when he finally released her. Just as quickly he turned away, and strutted back to his jeep.

"Oh, yeah. She's mine," he said smirking to himself.

Nikki backed out of the parking lot and headed toward the front gate. As she turned on the narrow road leading to her village, she realized she never got her mail from the post office.

Chapter Eight

God, she wanted to trust him. Surely, her heart couldn't deceive her twice in a lifetime. Surely, there was another man on this earth, besides her father, who was true blue until the end.

Nikki wanted to wear something tantalizing that would get his dander up. However, she knew with Will it wouldn't take much. Come to think of it, less clothing was what he wanted. She stepped over the pile of discarded rejects, on her way back to the closet.

Nikki finally decided on a cream-colored silk slip dress. Its simple sexiness intrigued her. Running her hands down the silkiness over her hips, she imagined his arms around her waist pulling her close to him. Nikki enjoyed the feel of the silk between her fingers.

She pulled her hair up with a silver and pearl clip, exposing every inch of her sensual neckline. Nikki put on her pearl earrings and bracelet. She touched up her makeup slightly, adding a bit of shine to her lips.

She picked up the pile of clothes on the floor, threw them in her closet, and pushed the door closed with her backside, trying to prevent any loose ends from escaping. Nikki ran her fingers up her calves, after sliding on her ankle strap sandals and then made her way downstairs.

Will arrived right on time. Hiding the peach tulips behind his back, he waited for Nikki to open the door. The sight of her electrified him. Her beauty made him tingle all over. It truly amazed him what a woman could do to herself in just four hours.

"My God, Nikki. You are gorgeous."

She smiled nervously as she stepped aside to let him in. He kissed her softly on the lips as he pulled the flowers from behind his back.

"Oh, Will. They're beautiful. Tulips are my favorite flowers." She went to the buffet to get a vase to put them in.

"They will be the perfect centerpiece for the table," she said to him sweetly.

"I wanted to pick something that reminded me of you," he said, as he caressed her cheek with the back of his hand.

"I love them. Thank you," she said, as she took his hand and led him into the den. "Why don't you sit here and let me get everything ready."

Will sat on the sofa and nervously rubbed his hands on his khaki pants. Sweaty palms never plagued him before. Something about her made him weak. Marines conditioned themselves to show no weakness or emotion. However, Nikki possessed a way of bringing all those things out in him. He wanted to love her...if she would only let him.

She entered the den and stood in front of him, taking his hand. Will rose slowly and put his arms around her waist.

"Dinner's ready," she told him.

"It smells wonderful," he told her as he pulled her closer.

"You don't smell so bad yourself."

She pulled away gently wanting to savor every moment with him.

Everything culminated in perfection. If Allison passed on nothing else to her daughter, she passed on her domestic talents. The perfectly chilled zinfandel filled both wine glasses to overflowing. Will inhaled deeply as he sat at his place at the table. His mouth began to water, as the aroma of the food filled his lungs. She raised her glass to his and clinked it gently.

"Thanks for coming," she said, lowering her eyes seductively.

"Thanks for asking," he told her, softly. Will took a bite of his meal. It absolutely melted in his mouth.

"Nikki, this is incredible!"

"I'm glad you like it."

Nikki ate slowly. It thrilled her to see him enjoying the dishes she prepared. *The way to a man's heart* – she thought to herself, regardless of how much she didn't want that to enter her mind. Now and again their eyes would meet, conversing silently together.

"Why don't you build a fire," she asked him, as she took the plates from his hands.

"Okay," he said. "Don't be too long."

Nikki cleaned up the mess quickly. She readied herself for the next part of the evening. Entering the den, she felt the gooseflesh rise on her arms, as she admired him bending over the fireplace. She walked toward him quietly. Without thinking, Nikki lowered herself to her knees and threaded her arms through his, wrapping them around his waist.

"You feel nice and toasty," she told him, laying her head against his back.

He could feel her breasts against him. Her scent made his heart race in his chest. He held her hands around him, and leaned into her.

"You make me feel that way," he told her dreamily.

Nikki squeezed him tightly. She realized how good it felt to have him close to her.

Sitting on the opposite end of the sofa, Nikki stretched her legs out across his lap. Will raised an eyebrow and gently rubbed the tops of her manicured feet. He really liked it when she was nice. He wondered what had gotten into her. He knew he'd like to get into her.

"Oooh, that feels good," Nikki told him, as she leaned back a little. "I could get used to this, you know."

"I was hoping you would. You bring out feelings in me I didn't know I had. I want to take care of you and protect you from everything."

"I don't want to be taken care of and protected, Will," she said frowning at him. "Don't you understand that I don't want to be controlled by any man, ever again?"

"I don't want to control you!" he said to her.

"I hate to say this, but I'm scared, Will," she finally told him.

He reached across and took her hand in his. "I know you are, Darlin'. I'm scared, too. Can't we just be scared together?"

"I didn't think Marines got scared," she said smiling at him, as she stroked his fingers with her thumb.

"There's a first time for everything, I reckon." He let out the breath he didn't realize he was holding. As he stood up from the sofa, he pulled her up to meet him. Wrapping his arms around her waist, Will pulled her close to him. She could feel her knees weaken as his warmth spread through her system.

"Give me a chance, Spunky."

Nikki laid her head on his chest. Closing her eyes, she savored his firm hands rubbing up and down her neck. Her heart rate quickened in her chest as she inhaled his extremely male aroma. Apprehensively, she ran her hands over his chest, feeling his muscles tense at her touch. Nikki felt his breath on the back of her neck making her shiver as she continued her massage.

Letting her previous concerns escape her mind, for now, she moved her hand to the warm, stiffening mound she had created in the front of his pants. She pressed her hand firmly on the throbbing rod that desperately wanted emancipation from the binding zipper of his jeans.

"Oh, God, Nikki," Will purred, as she continued to pleasure him.

Will ran his hand up her silky thighs, feeling the warm dampness between her legs. He slid one finger along the seam of her panties, until it easily slid under the material, to the hot flesh inside.

"God, you're so wet. You feel so incredible," Will said letting his finger caress her inner lips. The tiny nub ached with desire, as his fingers spread her lips, causing it to protrude further.

All the while, his erection increased, pushing harder into the denim. Nikki unbuttoned his fly and slowly lowered the zipper of his pants. She slid her hand into the opening of his underwear, grabbing hold of his thick shaft that now dripped with his juices. Her thumb slid over the dewy head causing his shaft to stiffen even more.

"Nikki, I don't know how much more I can stand," he told her as his hand continued to fondle her.

Nikki tilted her head back as his fingers entered her and his thumb continued rubbing the hot nub of her desire. She held on tightly to his shaft, moving up and down using his juice as a lubricant, to bring him to climax. She continued hanging on to him when her own orgasm took her by surprise.

"Will, I'm coming," she whispered.

She reared back in ecstasy, letting the wonderful pain of her climax pulsate through her body. As she fell back down to earth, she quickened her hand motions on Will's cock. He held onto her as his seed released over both of them. His breath hitched in his throat as he writhed with pleasure in her hands.

"Nikki, my Nikki," he said

"Yes, Will."

"You can really catch a guy off guard, you know?"

"That was my intention. I just couldn't stand it anymore. I wanted to see if you felt as good as I imagined."

"Well...did I pass the test?"

"Oh, yeah. You passed with flying colors."

✳ ✳ ✳ ✳ ✳

Will sat with his feet propped up on the desk and the newspaper splayed across his face when Boothe entered his office.

"Wake up!" Boothe said as he flung Will's feet from the desk and sat down in their place.

"What the hell do you want, Boothe?"

"Details. I know you've seen her. Are your balls still attached to your body?"

"You are damn funny, Boothe."

"Have you got into her pants yet?"

"Damn it! Is that all you think about?"

Boothe chuckled as he removed his cap. "What else is there?"

Boothe O'Brien was extremely handsome, but he knew it. He loved women and wasn't ashamed to show it. Both he and Will became instant friends once they began working together at Menwith Hill. Boothe enjoyed Will's quick wit. It seemed to get him out of trouble that he usually deserved.

Boothe complemented Will as well. Even though Will held more control over his loins than Boothe, the fact remained, Boothe proudly held the title of 'babe magnet'. Not only did he show interest in getting himself laid, but he wanted to make sure Will got laid, too.

"Why don't you go dig around in someone else's business and leave mine alone?" Will said irritably.

"What, is she frigid?"

"No, Boothe. She's not frigid."

"Okay, dude. I just hope you don't wait too long. A girl like that could make a man sit up and beg!"

"Don't I know it? I'm cooking dinner for her tonight. I thought I'd ask her to the Marine Corps Ball."

"You're cooking for her? Damn, man. You have got it bad, don't you?"

"I'm afraid so."

Chapter Nine

It took all the control Nikki could muster not to pick up the phone and call Will the next day. Determined not to appear a desperate woman, Nikki refused to give in to the urge, creating a knot in her stomach. So, later when she answered her ringing phone at work, relief spread through her body at the sound of his voice on the other end.

Despite her preoccupation, her work didn't suffer. Insomnia can be a blessing in disguise. When sleep escaped her, she focused her energies on the engineering designs Phil requested. They ended up being better than she anticipated. Phil congratulated Nikki in his office.

"This is exactly what the security department was interested in," Phil told her. "Keep this up, little girl, and you'll be promoted to chief engineer before the year is up."

"Thanks, Phil," Nikki replied. "It's amazing what a brain can come up with at 4:00 in the morning."

* * * * *

The wheels of the bright red convertible screeched loudly, as Nikki pulled into the driveway. Her father always scolded her for driving too fast. But, where does he think she got it? Will opened the front door, dishtowel thrown over one shoulder, laughing at her recklessness.

"You'd better slow down, Spunky!" he called to her.

She smirked at him as she grabbed her purse and got out of the car. Except for her father, no man ever nicknamed her. The term of endearment Will used warmed her heart. Once she reached the doorway, Nikki grabbed him around the neck and kissed him passionately.

"What's that for?" he asked her, a bit surprised.

"Just because I felt like it," she kissed him again deeply. Nikki removed the clip from her hair and shook it down to fall over her shoulders. Will reached for her and ran his fingers through the silky threads. It amazed him that this was the same woman who, just a few weeks ago, wanted to claw his eyes out. Every day she showed him another side of herself.

"Damn, you're beautiful!"

"I'm glad you think so," she told him pulling herself into him. She rubbed her hands up the back of his neck, massaging gently. Will pulled her hands toward his mouth, and kissed each one softly on the palm, before leading her to the den.

Surprisingly, the small home next door was neat and cozy. Having expected clothes thrown on the floor and dishes piled up in the kitchen, Nikki's look of astonishment pleased Will.

"We learn it in boot camp," answering her before the words could escape her mouth.

"I see that. I don't think I've ever been in a man's place that was tidier than my own."

"No offense, Darlin', but that's not saying much," he said snickering. "By the way, how many men's places have you been in anyway?"

"I don't think I'm gonna answer that since you decided on being such a smart-ass!" Nikki laughed when he smacked her on the butt.

Nikki bounced into the den and looked over the remainder of his surroundings. The sofa was a rich tan color with lots of cushions. She could imagine him relaxing there after a hard day's work. In each corner of the room, was an overstuffed chair in a complimentary plaid. One had a matching ottoman and the other sat next to a reading table. The opposite wall contained built-in bookshelves, packed to overflowing.

The dining room was temporarily his office. His computer sat on a small desk with the printer underneath. One small file cabinet was in the corner. Nikki enjoyed the rest of the tour as he led her into each room.

"This looks wonderful," she told him as she took in the sights and smells of his work.

Inhaling deeply, Nikki let the aroma of the food rush through her making her stomach rumble. Both plates contained hearty portions of chicken fried steak, mashed potatoes with cream gravy, and fried okra. Steaming biscuits awaited in a basket, next to two longneck bottles of beer.

In true southern fashion, Nikki dipped a huge piece of steak into the mashed potatoes, before putting it into her mouth. Will stared at her in shock as her cheeks puffed out from the mouthful. Covering her mouth with her hand, Nikki tried desperately to hold in her laugh of embarrassment.

"Nice manners, Darlin'," he said jokingly, as he wiped her mouth with his napkin.

"I'm sorry, but this is incredible. I've never been able to make good cream gravy. Did you do this all by yourself?"

"Yep, that's one thing my momma taught me how to do, make good gravy."

"Well, she did a fabulous job!" Nikki said before kissing him softly on the mouth.

* * * * *

They both laid back on the sofa to let their bloated stomachs settle.

"I have something I'd like to ask you," he said, as he took her hand in his. "The Marine Corps birthday is coming up in a few weeks and we always have a big shindig to celebrate. Do you think you'd like to go with me?"

"Oh, I'd love to go," squeezing his hand gently. Her hands began to tremble with a rush of excitement flowing through her veins.

Will turned to her and took her face in his hands. "You will be the most beautiful woman there."

"I don't even know what to wear."

"You've got plenty of time to find something. That's why I wanted to go ahead and ask you now, because I'm going back home for a few days for my parents' wedding anniversary. While I'm gone, you could call Missy, the Gunny's girlfriend, and she can go shopping with you. She's been to the ball the last two years and she can help you pick out what you need."

"Oh, Will, that'd be wonderful! I'll call her tomorrow. How long are you going to be gone?"

"I promised my mom I would stay at least a week. She just can't get enough of me, you know?"

Nikki just rolled her eyes as she said, "Yeah, I know the feeling."

They sat on his sofa with Will's arm around Nikki. She laid her head on his shoulder and rubbed her petite hands across the muscles of his thighs, feeling their firmness through his pants. Nikki's fingers inflamed him, as he tried to control his hard-on from projecting outwardly.

"I'll be thinking about you when I'm gone," he told her as he pulled her in closer.

"Yeah, you'll be thinking about me. Because I'm going to boost your memory," she said as she straddled him.

Nikki crushed her mouth on his, exploring every inch of his mouth with her tongue. Will moaned deeply in his throat as his cock pressed firmly on her sensual buttocks. She circled her hips in unison with his throbbing bulge.

"Nikki, I want to make love to you," he panted as she kissed him along his jaw line and down his throat.

"I know, Will. I want you, too. Maybe if you're a good boy while you're gone, I'll give you a surprise when you get home. I'm finding it harder and harder to keep my hands off you."

"I want your hands all over me, Darlin'. Every piece of me."

They unbuttoned and removed each other's shirt in unison. Will cupped her breasts feeling the heat coming off of her skin. He slid his hands around her back and quickly unhooked her bra. Her breasts bolted free of the garment, filling his hands completely.

"Damn, Nikki. You feel even softer than I dreamed," he took her nipple in his mouth and sucked it briefly, before turning to the other one.

Nikki pulled his nipples slightly making him groan with even more pleasure. She could feel his cock rubbing her pussy as she continued to pleasure herself on his mound.

"God, Will. Take your pants off. I can't stand it," she said lifting off of him.

She stepped out of her clothes and stood naked waiting for him to finish disrobing. Will sat back down on the sofa pulling her on top of him. His cock, slid through the pool of desire her pussy held for him. The head of his cock met her nub, and pulsated there briefly making her yelp with gratification.

"Yes, Will, make me come. I want to feel you come, too."

"Nikki. It won't take me long, Darlin'. You are so wet, I could come...right...now. Oh, God," he said as he released on her. Suddenly, her passion exploded with his. She rubbed herself over his cock, and climaxed. She fell on his chest. His cock continued to drip with desire, as he held her.

"God, Nikki. I am going to miss you."

"You damn well better," she said snickering.

✳ ✳ ✳ ✳ ✳

Will wiped the condensation from the bathroom mirror as his brother, Jake, barged into the bathroom.

"Oh, good! You're all nice and clean," Jake said. "Are you going somewhere?"

"Hey butthead, don't you knock?"

"I've seen everything you've got. Remember when you used to dance naked in front of the mirror when you were ten? And, when you were eleven you would count how many new pubes had sprouted overnight and measure if your rod had grown any. And, when you were thirteen, and you were practicing giving Cassandra Wiley the hot beef injection—"

"Okay, okay, so you've made your point. Growing up you didn't have a life of your own, so you had to gawk at me in my most private moments," Will said putting his little brother in a headlock. "I thought I'd go downstairs and have some of mom's chicken and dumplings."

"Oh, you can eat that tomorrow. I wanted to go to Huey's for a couple of beers and see if we can't pick up some chicks. You know Becky was sure giving you the eye at mom and dad's party last night. She and her friends will probably be there."

"I think I'll pass on Becky and her friends, but a few beers and some chow sounds good."

"Shit, the King is dead, or else he's turned queer. Which one is it, bro?" Jake asked accusingly.

"That, asshole, is my own damned business. But, I can tell you right now that I have not turned queer," Will said smirking.

"Oooh—Will's in love," Jake teased him. "So, who's the chick who's got you by the balls?"

"First of all, she's no chick. She's a woman I've been seeing."

"Mom's not going to like her. There is no girl good enough for her boys," Jake said mockingly.

"Why don't you go tell mom and dad that we won't be here for dinner, and let me get dressed."

"Okay, but don't take too long. I'm feeling lucky tonight," Jake said rubbing his hands together.

After pushing Jake out of the door, Will walked over to the closet to grab a shirt. That's when it hit him. *Nikki*. Her smell surrounded him as he pressed it up to his nose and inhaled deeply. Closing his eyes, the night she wore it flashed in his mind.

Sitting at the bar in the club on base sipping a beer, Will impatiently waited for Nikki to meet him after work. He grabbed a handful of pretzels and located her entrance in the mirror behind the bar. She radiated beauty unknowingly. A smile spread across his lips as he watched her search the room for him. When their eyes met in the reflection of the mirror, she smiled back at him seductively.

As Nikki leaned down to kiss Will on the cheek, his eyes followed the curve of her legs. The short black skirt she wore crept higher and higher up her silky thighs, as she situated herself on the stool.

"Damn, it's good to see you. I've been thinking about you all day," Will said, as he pulled her into him.

Staring deeply into his eyes, her breath caught in her throat when she began to reply. "I had a hard time trying to keep my mind on my work today, too. Why don't you order me a pint while I run to the ladies' room," she said kissing him again, innocently on the corners of his mouth.

"Your wish is my command."

As if time ran in slow motion, the next event took place. Simultaneously, Nikki jumped from the barstool as the waitress turned from the table of enlisted men behind them. The tray of half empty beer glasses crashed into Nikki's chest when they collided. Yelping, Nikki jumped back with her mouth agape.

"Holy Mary and Jesus!" Nikki said looking down at the practically new silk blouse now dripping with beer.

"Oh, my God! I am so sorry, love," the waitress said.

Will was absolutely useless as he stood in shock. Disgraced by his own arousal he gawked uncontrollably, at the silk blouse that now resembled an entry in a wet t-shirt contest.

"Jesus Christ!" Will blurted out covering Nikki with his jacket. The enlisted pricks at the table now noticed Nikki's full breasts, wet, round, and uncovered, as beer soaked into the fibers of the blouse. The lace bra she wore,

clearly visible now, accentuated the shape of her creamy cleavage. Her dark nipples were clearly apparent through the lace, and the chill from the beer, caused them to harden.

"Shit, Will, I'm going to have to change. Damn, I don't want to go all the way home and then come back though."

"Here, you can wear this. He took off his shirt and let her wear it."

Regardless of how many times the shirt had been to the cleaners, her scent remained.

Will's eyes fluttered as he returned to the present. He finished dressing just as his mother knocked on the bedroom door.

"It's open," Will called out as he buckled his belt.

At fifty-one, Mary Ann Chambers still radiated beauty, but with much more sophistication than she had in her twenties. She wore her dark hair, kissed with silver at her temples, down to frame her youthful face. She was slender, and still donned a bikini at the pool to keep her skin a healthy bronze.

She loved her boys and her husband more than life itself. When women's lib took over the sixties and many women joined the workforce to begin their careers, Mary Ann continued raising her family. In her mind, being a mother was her most important job. Will and Jake could always depend on their mother to be there when they got home from school, welcoming them with freshly baked cookies.

Mary Ann knew what her boys needed before they knew themselves. After twenty-eight years, nothing had changed. Mary Ann sensed that her oldest son had a secret, and she was determined to find out exactly what it was.

"Jake tells me that y'all aren't hanging around for dinner," Mary Ann said, as she entered the room.

"Yea, sorry. He wants to go pick up a girl."

"And you don't?"

"Nah, I don't think I'm up for that."

"When have you not been up for that?" Mary Ann asked as she rubbed her fingers over the short hairs above his ears.

At six-foot four, Will towered over his mother's five-foot two frame. He glowered down at her as she continued interrogating him.

"Have you met someone?"

"It's possible," he said smirking in the way his mother found adorable.

"Well, I'm happy to hear it. She must be pretty special if you're not interested in any women while you're here."

"She's scared of me."

"What in heaven's name for? You are the most harmless young man on earth," Mary Ann said showing her irritation.

"Apparently, she had her heart broken pretty badly. Let's just say she's a little gun shy."

"Oh. Well, you be sweet to her, like I know you will be, and maybe she'll come around," she said patting her son's cheek.

"That's what I plan on doing."

Chapter Ten

"What about this one?" Nikki asked Missy, holding up a silver strapless number.

"You need something to accentuate those God-awful gorgeous eyes of yours," she said as she fumbled through the racks of dresses. "Now this," she held up a lovely blue-green sequined evening gown, "this is perfect. Go try it on."

When Nikki came out of the dressing room every head turned. Elegance dripped from her as she turned around slowly, admiring the immaculate gown. It snugly accentuated her every curve. Missy was dead on. This one did bring out her eyes. Nikki hoped Will would be speechless. Adjusting the gold straps, her hands skimmed down the plunging neckline. Nikki turned to look at the back view as it draped seductively low down the length of her spine.

"Oh, Nikki. You look lovely. That's definitely the one," Missy said placing her hand over her mouth in admiration.

"Yes, it is, isn't it?" Nikki blushed as she noticed the other women in the shop staring at her. Giggling nervously, she stepped back inside the dressing room to change.

Will was right. Missy was the perfect shopping partner. No details were forgotten. Missy helped pick out the perfect shoes, handbag, and jewelry to accessorize Nikki's gown.

"The Marine Corps ball is magical," Missy told her. "You will never attend anything else like it. The pride and valor that the Marines have is astonishing."

Their friendship blossomed quickly. Missy recruited Nikki to help with the decorations. Every day after work Nikki happily went to Missy's house to help make centerpieces for the tables.

"I'm not supposed to tell you this," Missy told her, "but Garrett said Will has been a lot easier to work with since he met you."

"Really?" Nikki blushed.

"Yea, really. You can tell when a man has a good woman behind him. Now, the hard part is, convincing the man to see how fabulous the woman is."

"What do you mean by that?"

"Hell, I've been waiting for Garrett to figure out what a great catch I am now for two years! I still don't have a ring on my finger." She smiled as she continued curling ribbon with her scissors.

"Well, you said yourself, the Marine Corps ball was magical. Maybe it could be your lucky night." Nikki smiled as Missy raised an eyebrow at her.

"I won't hold my breath."

* * * * *

Nikki anticipated Will's return home. She, annoyingly, poised herself in front of the big bay window facing his house all morning long.

She proved a bit miffed when he didn't come over immediately. Now, two hours later, her aggravation turned into anger. Who the hell did he think he was? She'd be damned if she was going to wait around for him to decide when he was ready to see her. She just wouldn't be here whenever he got his sorry Marine ass up and over here!

Nikki's imagination was getting away from her as she began pulling on her boots, and grabbing her purse, to head out the door. Her chest heaved when the doorbell rang.

Her nipples pressed firmly against her t-shirt as she opened the door. Crossing her arms in front of her she awaited his brush-off. However, Will had other things in mind.

"Damn, you look good. I really missed you," Will told her as he scooped her into him as he walked across the threshold and kicked the door shut.

"Did you really? It took you long—" That was all she could get out before his mouth came down on hers.

His tongue played passionately with hers as a deep moan escaped from his chest. Chills ran up her spine as she relinquished to him, opening her lips wider so that he could delve in deeper. Will grabbed her waist with one hand and held the back of her neck with the other. His fingers wound around her silky locks as he pulled her into him.

Daylight no longer played between their bodies. They were now meshed together perfectly, as their hearts began beating in harmony.

Nikki felt the pressure of his loins pressing against her stomach. Her womb ached with desire, and the pressure became greater as each kiss deepened. Her hands smoothed across the muscles of his back, and down again resting finally on his firm buttocks. She held them there squeezing slightly as she pressed into him more than she thought possible.

Finally, after what seemed like hours, the two broke away for air. Will and Nikki stared at each other panting. Neither could believe the passion the other made them feel.

"I guess I missed you a little bit, too," Nikki said, placing her hand on her chest in an effort to lower her heart rate.

"God, Nikki. The things you do to me," Will said pulling her into him, pressing her head against his chest.

She stayed there feeling his heartbeat flutter in her ears. She inhaled his scent as her eyes closed with satisfaction. Feather kisses sprinkled the top of her head as he too savored the moment.

Chapter Eleven

Finally, the day of the ball arrived. Nikki was profoundly excited. She woke up early to help Missy set up the banquet room at the officer's club for the event. Around noon, they both looked over the room with satisfaction at the completed decorations.

Both women hurried to the beauty salon to spend the remainder of the afternoon being primped and pampered. Girlish laughter filled the salon as they sipped wine under the dryers. If nothing else, the Marine Corps ball firmly cemented Nikki and Missy's friendship.

✱ ✱ ✱ ✱ ✱

Will entered the gunnery sergeant's office.

"At ease, Will," Gunny told him as he turned in his chair.

"I've been given orders our regiment is to dispatch in a week to Heidelberg for a six month tour of duty. Apparently, they need our expertise getting past the language barrier. Your German is up to par?" he asked in German.

"Yes, sir," Will replied in the same language.

Will found early on in his military career language was his ace in the hole. He spoke fluent Spanish after living in Texas most of his life working for his father. Immigrants, straight from the border of Mexico, approached land development companies on a regular basis in hopes of finding employment.

After taking Spanish all through high school and in college, Will knew the basic aspects of conversation. However, after being around the workers every day, he picked up a few necessary coin phrases that kept him well liked and respected by the men.

Once in the Marine Corps, he quickly picked up German and Arabic. He prided himself on his ability to both speak and read all three languages. Will knew this 'additional skill' made his chances for advancement greater than the average Joe.

Will's heart sank at the thought of leaving Nikki. How could he tell her he had to go? This night must be perfect. Tomorrow he'd drop the ball.

"The girls aren't going to be happy about this," Gunny said, rubbing his brow.

"No, sir."

"We'll have to make tonight count for something. Go make yourself handsome and we'll discuss this more on Monday."

"Thank you, Gunny," Will said as he turned to leave the office.

* * * * *

Nikki's nerves were shot to hell. She wanted to take Will's breath away. Feeling sexy and alive, she made final touches to her makeup before putting on her dress.

Right on time, she thought to herself looking at her watch when the doorbell rang.

"Come in, Will," she yelled down to him.

He opened the door and walked in.

"I'll be down in just a second," Nikki called to him. Wanting to make an entrance, she made one final check in the full-length mirror, twirling side to side to view every angle.

Will swallowed the lump in his throat as Nikki gracefully came down the stairs. Her long legs peeked out of the slit up the side of her gown. The sequins of the dress made her eyes sparkle even more than usual. His sweaty palms made it difficult to hold the bouquet of Gerber daisies he held behind his back.

She grabbed hold of the banister when she caught sight of him. A man in uniform is one thing. Will in his dress blues was breathtaking. Her knees buckled as she tried to make her way down the stairs without falling. Her dry mouth stuttered when she opened it to speak.

"Will, you are so handsome," she said, her voice quivering when she spoke. "I'm so lucky to have such a fine-looking escort."

"I would say I was the lucky one," he said as he pulled her into him, and kissed her deeply.

"Are you hiding something?" she asked as she peeked behind him.

"Just a little something," he said as he brought out the flowers. He had requested the florist cut one of the flowers into a wrist corsage that he placed on her slender arm.

"Oh, Will, you don't miss a trick do you? I never knew a Marine could be so romantic."

"You haven't seen anything yet." He opened the door and led her down the porch. At the end of the drive awaited a black Rolls Royce, complete with chauffeur.

"Oh my God! I can't believe you did all this."

"You deserve it. I want you to feel like a queen tonight."

She slipped her arm through his as they walked to the car. Her heart pounded in her chest as the chauffeur took her hand and helped her in. Will went around to the other side of the car and slid in next to her.

Nikki grabbed on to his white-gloved hand and squeezed tightly. She could feel the tears saturate her eyes as she basked in the moment. Pulling a tissue out of her handbag, Nikki blotted her eyes as Will turned her face to his.

"I think I love you, Nikki." *He couldn't leave for Germany without telling her.* "I just want you to know that. No matter how I've tried to fight it. I can't, Darlin'. You're it for me. I know this is sudden and all, but I just feel like I needed to tell you."

"Oh, Will." The tears came full force then. "God, I can't believe I'm blubbering like a fool. I can't believe all of this. I do feel like a queen. You are the most incredible man I've ever known."

He put his arm around her as she nestled into him. Nikki didn't say the three words he so desperately needed to hear. Hadn't he just poured his heart out to her? He wanted to give her all the love that filled his soul. She loved him. This he knew. She was the one who was not ready to accept it.

They traveled most of the way in an awkward silence. Nikki couldn't help wondering what bothered him. Surely something did, because he never suffered a loss for words. The chauffeur smiled at her in the rear view mirror as they pulled onto the base.

"Wait right here," Will told her as they stopped in front of the officer's club. Whatever it took, he would make her belong to him. Tonight would be their night. Nikki Phillips would let him into her heart. It would break his heart if she didn't.

The chauffeur opened the car door, but Will's hand reached out for her. She grabbed hold of him and stepped out of the car.

"Have a lovely evening," the chauffeur told them. "Midnight, sir?"

"Yes, we'll meet you right here," Will said. He tucked his white hat under his arm as they entered the ballroom. His eyes darkened as they barely peeked from under the brim. He stared into her eyes, both seductively and dangerously.

Nikki looked around the room for Missy and Garrett. Missy spotted her first and came across the floor in record speed.

"You look amazing," Missy told her as she played with one of the tendrils of hair Nikki left dangling down the back of her neck.

"You look wonderful, too."

"Well, Will, did we meet your approval?" Missy kissed him on the cheek and slipped her arm in his unoccupied one as he led them toward their table.

"It doesn't take much to make her look radiant," he said as he squeezed Nikki's hand with his forearm. Will took her through the ballroom introducing her to a few of his fellow Corps member friends. She gawked at the sight of so many beautiful people in one room. Nikki could imagine her mother feeling exactly this way when she and her father first started dating.

Across the aisle was Boothe O'Brien, with a blond piece of arm candy, hanging on him.

"Nikki, you remember Boothe?"

"Hey, Nikki. This is Trixie," Boothe said in his deep Georgian accent. "You've been keeping my boy Will here from poker night. Did you know that?"

"No, I didn't," she said blushing at the thought of him turning down his friends to be with her. She couldn't help wondering if Will ever dated bimbos like the one Boothe had latched onto him. That man oozed sex appeal from every pore in his skin. Surely, he could find a nice, respectable date. Nikki believed Boothe just wanted the best fuck of the evening, and Trixie must be it.

"What are you going to do when Will goes—" Boothe's words were cut off by a punch on the back by Will.

"Shut up, Boothe," he said turning to Nikki. "Come on, we had better get to our seats. They'll be serving soon."

Nikki could feel the tension rising between them. *What was Boothe going to say to her?* Will seemed slightly preoccupied. Nikki wondered what was bothering him. What was he keeping from her?

"Are you okay?" Nikki looked over at him as they sat down.

"I'm fine. Boothe is one of my best friends but he can be a little too much sometimes," he said as he kissed her on the cheek. "Would you like to dance?"

"I've been waiting for you to ask me," Nikki said as she stood with him. She wasn't sure he was telling her the whole truth, but she intended to find out.

Nikki felt like Cinderella when Will held her close as they danced. Will certainly looked as handsome as Prince Charming. Almost to the point of pinching herself, Nikki tried to convince herself this wasn't a dream. It was real. He was real, and so was his love for her. Joy surged through her body as they glided across the dance floor. His gaze pierced through her making her chest tighten.

She needed to tell him. Love filled her completely at just the thought of him, but her stupid lack of courage banned those tiny words from passing through her lips. Nikki didn't realize how her silence ripped through him, like a sword in the heart. If she understood, she would have said what he wanted to hear.

It took every ounce of control to swallow the lump in his throat, and stop his heart from breaking.

Nikki took his breath away every time he looked at her. He loved everything about her. He loved the way her skin felt under his fingers. He loved the way she wore just enough perfume to entice him. He loved the way she squeezed his hand when she was nervous. He loved the way her long neck beckoned him to kiss every inch of it. God, how he loved her.

Chills escalated up her spine as the low harmony of the bagpipes played the Marine Corps Hymn. Traditional Corps pomp and circumstance topped off the evening. Following the bagpipe player came the color guard, marching through the ballroom, chanting as they passed. Gunny acknowledged several high officers from visiting bases with jokes and toasts enjoyed by all.

"There is someone else I would like to recognize, if you would all give me the chance to do so," Gunny said as he stepped down from the podium.

Quietly, the bagpipes played a Scottish love song as Gunny made his way to Missy.

"Many of you know this evening wouldn't have gone off as magnificently as it did without the help of my lovely girlfriend, Missy," he said taking her hand in his and kissing it softly. "This woman has stood by me and put up with the Corps mentality for two and half years. Now, I'm asking her to do me the honor of becoming a proper Marine Corps wife."

The crowd cheered as Missy wiped the tears that were streaming down her face.

"Garrett, yes, oh yes! It's about damn time," she said throwing her arms around him, as the entire room filled with laughter and tears.

Garrett placed an enormous diamond ring on Missy's finger as he pulled her to him. He kissed her hard, as all the women in the room blotted their eyes, and all the men smiled. Soon, the clock struck twelve and Cinderella knew her evening must come to an end.

They stopped by the photographer's table before leaving the club. If nothing else, a picture to remember this night would belong to him. Will took her hand, and they walked outside into the crisp night air.

✳ ✳ ✳ ✳ ✳

"Do you know how proud I was to have you on my arm tonight?" He embraced her tightly, as they walked in her house.

"Do you know how proud I was to be there with you? I have never felt so special in my entire life, Will. Thank you for everything."

"You never answered me, Nikki," he told her as he kissed each side of her neck.

Confusion spread over her face as she questioned him with her eyes.

"I told you I love you. I mean it, Nikki. You are everything to me. I think you feel the same way. If you don't, then please tell me now. If you do, then don't be afraid. Tell me, Darlin'. I want to hear you say it."

"Oh, Will," she said as she threw herself into his arms. "I can't tell you how much you mean to me. I can't imagine not having you in my life. You make me feel like I am the most important thing in your life and I treasure that. But I'm afraid of love, Will. I want to know when I say the words; you will know how truly deep they go for me. I've got to get over these hang-ups keeping me from telling you all I feel. Just know I want you forever and you are the only one I want."

"That's not the same as loving me." Will told her looking disappointedly in her hazy eyes. "I'll accept it for now, but one day soon you're going to have to admit that I am the love of your life."

"For now, Will, just know that this has been the best night of my life."

Will scooped her up and kissed her madly.

"The night's not over yet," he whispered.

Will's mind concentrated on Nikki's sumptuous mouth. Completely caught in the moment, Will wasn't watching where he was walking. He tripped on the floor mat catapulting both of them across the floor. They laughed hysterically when they both ended up sitting on the bottom of the steps. Nikki landed on top of him sitting on his lap. Staring down at him as he began caressing her back, she seductively pulled her dress up to her thighs so she could straddle him and then bent down to kiss his lips. Nikki placed her hands on his neck and ravaged his mouth with her tongue.

The hardness of his arousal pressed against her as she dove deeper and deeper. He slid his strong hands under her dress and rubbed the top of her thighs. How he had longed to hold her just this way. They kissed for what seemed like an eternity. Will slowly moved his hands higher under her dress feeling her creamy skin as he went.

"God, I want you, Nikki. If you want me to stop, tell me now. I don't know how much longer I can hold myself back."

"I don't want you stop, Will. I want to feel you…all of you." Nikki could wait no longer. She needed him to take her tonight.

Lifting herself off of him, she gently took his hand and led him upstairs to her bedroom. His erection protruded through his dress pants. Nikki unbuttoned his jacket and slid it over his shoulders. Knowing the Marine in him would cringe if she threw it on the floor, she draped it carefully on the back of the chair by her window.

Unbuttoning his shirt, Nikki's fingers worked their way slowly beyond Will's undershirt and over his hairy chest. Her whole body tingled as she followed the trail down to his navel. She massaged the muscles on his chest and abdomen. Nikki pulled him to her and kissed him hard and long.

Will's erection throbbed under the starched material. He slid the delicate straps down her shoulders and continued sliding her dress over her hips until it fell to the floor. Nikki stepped out gracefully and removed the clip from her hair letting it cascade over her creamy shoulders. He threaded his fingers through it as they kissed deeply. Her taut nipples suffered in need as Will gently sucked each one before moving back up to her mouth.

Once unbuttoned, his erection burst forth with freedom, as she let his pants fall to the floor. The pain eased in his loins as her fingers slid around to squeeze his buttocks. Will moved his hands down the back of her lace panties and cupped her bottom. Her voluptuous body poured over him.

Will lowered himself to his knees and kissed at the top of her panties, pulling them down slightly and kissing lower to the line of soft curly hairs that covered her. Nikki moaned deep in her throat as he pulled her panties all the way down.

"I have dreamed about you every night, just like this," he told her softly leading her to the bed.

"You have been in my dreams, too."

She lay down on the bed and brought him to her. Kissing her deeply, he reached underneath her back to bring her closer. Will loved the feel of her breasts against him. Her hard nipples rubbed against his making heat rush through his body. She could feel his desire pressing firmly on her stomach leaving a slight trail of his juices as evidence of his desire. Reaching down, he let his hands drown in the slickness between her legs. "God, you feel incredible," he told her, rubbing the tiny nub that tingled with desire for him. The rush of excitement soared through her veins as his talented fingers brought her to orgasm. Will gently entered her in slow fluid movements. She pulled him into her, deeper, as she wrapped her long legs around his waist. He plunged inside her again and again, as the heat rose between them. They came together, in a surge of adrenaline and need. His liquid desire filled her completely, as he continued to convulse inside her.

Nikki held him close to her as she kissed his chest softly. Will's tongue slid slowly down her neck to her breasts flicking each nipple gently to firmness.

"I have never had a man make me feel like that, Will. I have never been taken so completely," she said blushing.

He rolled off her onto his elbow, and rested his head in his hand. He let his fingers glide across her milky smooth breasts. She reached over to him and played with the dark hairs that covered his chest muscles.

"I'm glad that I'm the only one, Nikki," he told her as he kissed her softly on the nose.

"Will you stay with me tonight?" she asked him as she brought her hand to his face. "There's no place I'd rather be, Darlin'." He pulled her into him and kissed her mouth hard. Will rolled onto his back with her head nestled under his arm. Wrapping their arms around each other, Nikki crossed her leg over his. Quietly, they drifted off to sleep.

Chapter Twelve

When Will awoke, Nikki's deep blue-green eyes were staring back at him. Her fingers played with the hairs on his chest making his body tingle as they moved up and down his torso. The sunlight through the window highlighted her hair. He couldn't remember ever seeing anything more breathtaking.

"Good morning," she said to him as she continued stroking his chest.

"Good morning, beautiful," he replied as he raised his hand to stroke her silky hair. "Did you sleep well?"

"Never better."

He kissed her gently on the tip of her nose. She smiled at him with a vulnerability he adored. They lay there not speaking, just caressing each other softly. When he ran his fingers down her back he could feel the goose pimples pop up on her arms and legs. She shuddered as he continued stroking her up and down. Will could feel his pulse start to race as she scooted closer to him.

Nikki massaged his chest and then let her hand run down his hip to the top of his thigh. She stopped there and massaged gently the hard hamstring on the back of his leg. Will's hand cupped her breast as he flicked her nipple with his thumb. Nikki felt his desire pressing against the puddle forming between her legs.

He kissed her deeply as he gently connected them, entering her fully as she wrapped her leg across his thigh. The squeak Nikki let out slightly as he thrust himself into her harder made Will shiver. She could feel him tremble as he began to climax. Joining his ecstasy, she came to his liquid heat filling her completely. The moan deep in his throat echoed as he continued to throb inside her. Nikki held him there tightly as she kissed his neck and nestled her head into his chest.

"God knows I love you, Nikki."

* * * * *

Nikki walked into the bathroom just as he was wrapping a towel around his waist. His muscular legs looked even more irresistible when the hairs on them were beaded with water. She leaned over and kissed him briefly on the lips.

He went into the bedroom, dressed and went downstairs to make the coffee. By the time Nikki got downstairs Will was already buried in the newspaper.

"Do you want to tell me what's bothering you, yet?" she asked him as she walked in the den with her coffee.

"How do you know that something is bothering me?" he asked frowning at her.

"Mainly because I care about you and I can tell that something's up."

"There is something that I need to talk to you about. I just didn't want to ruin last night."

Nikki felt the pain in her chest as her imagination ran amok thinking of all the horrible scenarios that could be causing him such distress.

"I have to leave for a while, Nikki. You know the Marines can send me anywhere at anytime."

Nikki swallowed hard as the pain radiated to her throat.

"Where are they sending you and for how long?"

"To Germany for six months."

"Six months? Oh, God," she said as she tried to hold back the tears. "Will, things were just starting to feel right between us."

"Nothing has to change, Nikki. I swear I'm coming back to you. You have to believe that."

"When do you have to leave?"

"In four days."

"We only have four days? How long have you known about this?"

"I found out yesterday morning. I told you I didn't want to say anything to you last night to ruin your evening…our evening."

Nikki sat quietly as she tried to absorb everything he just told her. She wanted to go with him, but her contract bound her for at least the next two years. The holidays wouldn't be the same without him, but now he would be somewhere else, alone.

"You'll be gone at Christmas?"

"I'm afraid so, Nikki. I'm sorry. You know there is nothing I can do about this. This is what I've been trained to do."

"I know, Will. I don't blame you. It's just not fair, that's all."

"I know. God, I don't want to leave you, but I don't have a choice."

"Now it's all making sense. This is why you were so uptight when Boothe was talking to me. He wanted to know what I was going to do when you left. Garrett? Is he going too? Is that why he wanted Missy to marry him before he left?"

"Yes, he has to leave Missy behind, too. He wanted to leave her as his wife, not just his girlfriend."

"Why can't he take her with him if they're married?"

"Nikki, there will be four guys bunking up in one room together. There wouldn't be room for her there. No woman would want to share a room with four Marines, trust me."

"No, I guess not. I wonder how Missy is taking the news."

"I'm sure no better than you are," he said as he pulled her to him, and held her tight.

"I'll be back before you know it, Darlin'," Will said trying to smile.

"Six months. That's a long time. I hope you don't forget about me."

"Nikki, I don't lie. If the words leave my mouth, then it's the truth. I mean it when I say I love you. I mean it when I say I'll come back to you. I swear on my life."

"And I mean it when I say that I'll be waiting for you," Nikki told him as he held her tightly.

Chapter Thirteen

He paused in front of his bedroom and smiled at her slyly. His unmade bed was large and welcoming. On his nightstand sat an alarm clock and a sci-fi novel. They sat down on the bed together.

"Stay here with me tonight, Nikki," he asked her as he held tightly onto her hand.

"I don't know. We both have to be at work tomorrow," she told him as she laid her head on his shoulder.

"I won't keep you up late, Marine Corps promise. I just want to feel you next to me, all night. We won't have many more nights together for a while."

"How can any woman in her right mind say no to you?"

"I don't rightly know, but somehow they have managed to," he said grimacing when she punched him in the arm.

"I'll need to go home and get a few things."

"Get on with yourself, then," he replied, before kissing her thoroughly.

Will watched through his window as she hurried back to her house. He laughed and shook his head as he watched the door close. How did she get to him so quickly? He couldn't stand the thought of sleeping alone after being with her. However, the thought of her witnessing one of his dreaded nightmares plagued him, making him apprehensive.

They went to bed early that evening. The romp in the hay they both wanted would have to wait for another day. Nikki waited for him in bed. Will spooned her backside into his naked crotch. She snickered as the furry hairs protecting his cock tickled her buttocks. Her cunt began to soften and dampen with the touch of him so close. He kissed her softly on the ear and whispered, "I'm glad you stayed."

"I'm glad you asked me to," she whispered back.

Nikki relished the idea of spending the night without engaging in sexual activity. She scooted into him further, and he wrapped his arms tightly around her body. His warm breath on her neck comforted her, as he slowly drifted to sleep. Nikki closed her eyes and let his heartbeat lull her into dreams.

✳ ✳ ✳ ✳ ✳

You don't think about the mutilated and charred bodies until a tank battle is over.

Will and his crew came across an Iraqi who made it a few hundred yards from his bombed out convoy before he fell in a heap. Dying alone in the desert for a barrel of crude pulled at Will's emotions.

Lifting the Iraqi, his comrades looked through the back of his head and out of his eye sockets. Napalm was vicious. It made a man's brain pop out like popcorn.

Will bolted upright breathing heavily as he came out of the dream.

"What is it, Will?" Nikki asked, reaching out to comfort him.

"Nothing," he replied jerking away at her touch.

Will stood, pulling his boxers on and walking toward the window. He couldn't tell her. She would think he was crazy. He wasn't so sure that he wasn't. What normal guy wakes in a cold sweat almost every night from nightmares? Shit, he should have stopped doing that when he was eight.

Nikki approached him putting her hands on his back. She could feel him trembling. His skin felt cold and clammy to her touch.

"Look, Nikki. I'm all right," he told her as he started to walk into the bathroom. "I just need to splash some cold water in my face."

Nikki hurt for him and he knew it. She didn't understand what had just happened, but it wasn't good. Something terrified him, something he wouldn't share with her. How could he say he loved her, but not open up completely to her?

Nikki didn't stay in bed when she heard the faucet of the shower come on. Making her way into the kitchen, she paused by the den and picked up his jacket that lay across the sofa. Bringing it up to her face, she inhaled deeply. His scent made her tingle all over.

Will came downstairs and fixed himself a cup of coffee.

"I'm sorry, Darlin'," he told her as he pulled her close to him. "There are just some things I'm not ready to share. War is hell, you know?"

"If you truly love me as much as you say you do, you should be able to tell me anything."

"Yea, I know. I will someday. Just not today," he said as he fixed himself a cup of coffee.

"You always want me to spill my guts. What makes it different with you?"

Nikki tried to overlook the strange look in his eyes. Instead, she focused on the rest of him. A man in uniform excited her beyond belief. Maybe it was just her man in uniform. Even his fatigues turned her on. She loved the way his muscles rippled under the cuffs of his sleeves. She had watched him last night as he meticulously folded and ironed each one to perfection. His boots radiated the tedious spit-shine Will performed on them. The smell of leather, shoe polish and aftershave made her breathless.

"You know how you can't tell me that you love me? You just can't? Well, I just can't share this with you. Let's just leave it at that," he told her as he gulped from his cup. He finished the last of his coffee, and put his cap on his head.

"The only difference here, Will, is that I understand there are things you can't talk about. Daddy was the same way. I just don't want to be punished because of what you think I should tell you. If I don't tell you that I love you, then you're never going to open up to me?"

"It has nothing to do with that. I respect the fact that you can't tell me now. I don't want you to tell me something you don't mean just to make me feel better. I have explained my feelings for you, but this is something I just can't talk about. I'm sorry, but I've got to go." He leaned in to kiss her good-bye but she pulled away, quickly.

"It always ends up being about control." She turned to go upstairs and get her things. Will grabbed her by the arm and jerked her around to face him.

"The only person trying to control this situation is you, Nikki," He then turned and walked out the door.

* * * * *

Will tried to call Nikki several times that same day, but just got her voice mail. He left several messages, but received no reply. *She must be really busy or still ticked,* he told himself.

"So how's the babe?" Boothe asked Will as he spotted him during the fifty chest presses Will completed, religiously, every day.

"Fine."

"What do you mean, fine? I thought you two were attached at the hip?"

"I haven't talked to her today. I've left a thousand messages, but she hasn't called me back."

"Did you fuck her yet? Maybe you are not as much of a lady's man as you think you are. So, that would make you available to play poker tonight."

"Why do I even hang out with you? All you do is give me grief," Will replied grunting with the exertion it took to press the last ten.

"I'm just trying to keep you level headed that's all. It looks to me like you're pussy whipped! What was up with you jack-slapping me the other night? She was going to find out we were leaving sooner or later. I was just trying to help you out, that's all."

"Shit! I certainly couldn't live without that," Will said rather sarcastically. "Yeah, I'll play poker tonight. I would really like to kick your ass."

Will pushed himself beyond the point of exertion. Sweat dripped from his nose and chin as he tried to rid the nagging ache she created from his chest. *Maybe he was turning into a pussy!* Big deal if she hadn't called him today. She did have a life and so did he for that matter. *Shit, he was whipped! When did that happen?*

Later that night Will set his gym bag by Boothe's front door.

He threw on the spare clothes he kept in Boothe's barracks. Boothe went to the commissary to load up on snacks and beer. By the time he returned, Will had almost talked himself out of staying and was going home to hash it out with Nikki.

"Where are you headed?" Boothe asked him.

"I don't think I'm up to this tonight after all."

"Well, if you can't hang out with your buddies anymore, then you have it worse than I thought."

"She doesn't have any say over me. I can do whatever I want. Count me in," Will sneered as he grabbed a beer from the fridge.

"Chill out, Dude. "

"One day, Boothe, you're going to have a chick have a hold on your balls and you'll know what I mean."

"Oh, no. No chick will ever have me by the balls unless she's waiting on me to come."

"You are a pig, Boothe."

"Ante up, you pussies," Boothe barked at the circle of men around the table. Will had never lost a game to Boothe before; tonight his head remained up his ass the entire game. One hand after another he forked over more and more money to his smart-ass friend. Boothe reveled in the notion that he took everyone for all they had. Once the last of his money was turned over to Boothe, Will slammed his cards on the table clinking beer bottles against each other on his right and left.

"I've had it. You've got all my money, asshole. I'm out of here."

"Oh, don't go away mad, Will," Boothe said sarcastically. "Just go away. I'm sick of seeing your "run over puppy" look anyway. Why don't you just run back to ball crushing Nikki, fuck her, and get over it. You obviously can't live without her," he quickly yelled, trying to get the last word in before Will slammed the door.

Chapter Fourteen

The entire day Nikki tried to focus on the project she was working on. *I'm not trying to control him. I am not the controlling person here.*

Nikki sat on her bed finishing one longneck after another waiting for Will to come home. He always beat her home.

She startled at the sound of her doorbell. It continued to ring over and over again. She groggily rubbed her eyes and looked over at the clock. She must have cried herself to sleep. The room was dreadfully dark and quiet except for the sound of the doorbell and the pounding at her front door.

"I know it's you, Will. What on earth could you possibly have to say to me?" She opened the door.

He looked like a whipped puppy. Lack of sleep left dark circles under his eyes. *Too bad,* she thought to herself. *I hope you never sleep again!*

"Can I come in?" he asked her.

"I don't know why I should let you in," she tried to hold back the tears but one escaped and slid down her cheek.

"Oh, God, Nikki. Please don't cry."

She turned and walked into her den leaving the front door open. He came in quietly and closed the door behind him. She sat on the sofa and pulled her knees into her chest holding a pillow in front of her.

"Damn it, Nikki. Listen to me!" Will yelled at her, as he grabbed her arm.

"Get your freaking hands off of me, you asshole!"

"Not until you listen to me," he shouted at her.

"You don't have anything to say that I want to hear!"

"Nikki quit being so damned hardheaded and listen to me!"

"Damn, Nikki, I love you." Will felt the knotting in his stomach as he continued, "I can't bear to see you cry like this knowing I'm the one that caused it. I don't want to fight with you. I just need a little more time, that's all.

"There are a lot of things that men, especially military men don't discuss. Their feelings are first and foremost on that list. I've been in war more than once, Nikki. Unfortunately, that can really screw with your head. If I were going to share it with anyone it would be you. I just have to figure it out for myself before I can let you in. Sometimes I don't know what's wrong with me, Nikki. What if I hurt you and didn't know what I was doing? War veterans do that a lot I'm told. I couldn't live with myself if I ever hurt you, Darlin'."

"I wasn't expecting this, Will." Nikki rubbed the tears from her eyes as she looked up at him. "I guess I didn't understand how tough this is for you. I didn't mean to be such a bitch. I just don't like to see you hurting inside. I want to help you. I'll try my best to give you some room. By the way, my daddy taught me some moves so if you ever do try to hurt me in my sleep, I'll be ready for you," she said laughing now.

He kissed her softly on the lips. Her tears fell down her cheeks to her mouth. He could taste the salt as he continued to kiss her tears away.

"Do you trust me, Spunky?"

"Yes."

"Then let me take you upstairs and let me show you how much you mean to me."

* * * * *

Nikki dabbed at the tears in her eyes as Missy and Garrett kissed for the first time as husband and wife. She stood next to Missy as her maid of honor, with Will serving as the best man. Nikki remembered Roxie's wedding four years ago.

That marriage ended in heartbreak, not to anyone's surprise. John was an asshole. There was no sugarcoating it. He treated Roxie like trash. When Aaron was born, nothing changed. If anything, things got worse. That's when Roxie filed for divorce and decided to support herself and her son, as best she could.

Nikki hoped that Garrett and Missy would have a happier life together. Starting a marriage apart for six months could be good or a hindrance, depending on how you looked at it.

Missy looked absolutely stunning. She and Nikki had gone shopping the day before to find her the perfect dress. Garrett made all the preparations at the church and for a small reception at the club on the base. Missy needed to find something suitable to wear in just a few hours.

Luckily, the first shop they entered carried just the thing. It was simple, but dazzling nonetheless. She picked an ivory satin a-line gown, with a beautifully scalloped neckline, beaded with pearls. The pearls continued down the back where a sheer scarf draped to the floor. It fit her perfectly. She found a simple shoulder length veil with blusher that she placed over her upswept hair. Nikki found a similar dress in peach that she chose for herself. She added a few sprigs of baby's breath to her hair that she removed from her bouquet.

Nikki's pulse accelerated as she glanced across the aisle to see Will looking at her. Nikki smiled at him sweetly and looked down at her flowers.

Will stood at ease behind Gunny. Nikki could see him rolling the rings around in his hand as he listened to the minister. *Someday*, he thought to himself, *we will be standing in front of everyone pledging our love to each other*. He winked at Nikki when he saw her eyes searching for his. Her stomach fluttered as she inconspicuously brought her fingers to her lips and blew a kiss his direction.

The reception was simple, but included plenty of alcohol. Nikki sipped champagne as Will went to the bar to get a beer.

"We've made our appearance. Let's get out of here," Will told her after the cake was served.

"God, I was hoping you were ready. I can't see you in that uniform and not want to rip it off of you," she whispered.

"Shit. Hurry, before I jump you right here," Will said pulling her out of the reception.

* * * * *

"Again," she purred at him as she nuzzled his neck with her nose.

"I think I've created a monster," Will said covering his face with his hands.

"Look, Bud. You're the one leaving so you need to make up for all the wild sex you *won't* be having while you're gone. Let me just remind you, women are off limits. I don't care what Boothe O'Brien tries to tell you."

"You could make even Boothe O'Brien beg for mercy, Darlin'. But, we won't give him the chance. Here, I have a little something for you," he told her as he took her hand. He slid it under the covers and placed it on his very hard cock.

"Damn, Will. Little is not the word I would use for you," she fondled him gently, as she felt herself heat with desire.

He pulled her on top of him, lifting her up so he could take her breast in his mouth. He suckled her and laved her with kisses as she writhed with passion. Her nipples hardened more with every flick of his tongue. She pressed his head into her breasts even more as he continued to suckle.

The coarse hairs between his legs tickled the delicate skin on the inside of her thighs. She shivered with each movement as his cock pressed firmly on her inner lips. Her slickness aroused him tremendously, and he entered her fully. His thick cock pressed against her inner walls, making her wriggle with desire and push his shaft even deeper into her.

"God, Will. Your body has to be the most incredible thing I have ever felt," She pulled on his erect nipples and caressed the indentation between his chest muscles.

Will pulled out of her and flipped her over onto her stomach. She raised herself slightly and held onto the headboard. Her ass taunted him as she circled it, beckoning him to enter her again. He thrust his hard shaft into her and pulled her by the waist back into him even more. She continued to writhe in circular motions to his every thrust. Pulling herself up by the headboard, she came violently, purging her juices with every thrust of his cock.

"Nikki, Nikki..." Will moaned as he too emptied himself into her. She could feel the heat of his ejaculation spread through her body. He rested against her holding her by the waist and resting his head along her spine. His pulsating cock continued to trickle his seed as he remained inside her hot, wet, pussy.

They collapsed, both spent, Will on top of her still filling her. And, that's how they stayed, until his erection subsided and finally slid out of her. Somewhere in the night, he rolled to the side of her and she spooned her backside into him to sleep the remainder of the night.

Chapter Fifteen

Nikki's heart heaved in her chest. She and Missy waved to Will and Gunny as they stepped on the bus. Missy had experienced this several times before with Garrett. After living together for over a year, it was common to be separated for weeks at a time.

"You better get used to this if you're going to be a Marine's wife," she told Nikki, slipping her arm through hers.

"You're rushing things just a bit, don't you think?"

"I can see it in his eyes, Nikki. I've known Will for a long time and have never seen him have that look with another woman. Trust me. He's hooked!"

Nikki smiled nervously as they got into her car. Missy seemed way too calm. Nikki wondered if her strength was just a façade. She was probably bucking up so Nikki wouldn't break down. They spoke few words on the drive home. Missy twirled the ring that now adorned her hand around her finger, as she delighted in the fact she was now Garrett's wife. Finally.

True to rumor, the Marine Corps ball was magical.

When Nikki didn't slave over her work, she spent her time at *The Joiner Arms* or with Missy. She didn't return home until late. She didn't enjoy the thought of being alone. *When did I become such a sap?* She swore a man wouldn't trap her again. But, she fell into Will's net just the same. He consumed her soul. To be with him, hold him, and yes, to love him, even though she wasn't ready to say it out loud, would complete her.

Will spent what little spare time left to him writing her. He somehow felt closer to her when he put pen to paper. It became almost therapeutic to sit quietly by lamplight, having long conversations as if she were right there with him. He would lie awake at night and try to imagine her voice over the snoring and other bodily noises of his comrades.

Will called her every Sunday night at nine o'clock on the dot. It was down time for both of them, so being able to share the events of the week at that time was comforting. It aggravated Nikki knowing each Sunday evening she sat like a schoolgirl anxiously awaiting the ringing telephone from her beau.

Nikki loved the sound of his voice on the line. She could feel the moistness it created between her legs. Cold showers became second nature to her after being on the phone with Will for any length of time. Her heart pounded, her palms would sweat, her breathing would quicken by the minute, before, during and after his call.

Nikki possessed Will's heart for now and always. Usually, several Marines stood in line to use the base phone. Will's ears suffered the groans and complaints yelled if he took longer than they deemed necessary. Therefore, the little time they had was quality time. He would whisper his thoughts about what he planned to do to her once they were together again. He was careful not to let his fellow Marines hear what he said, or notice his erection forming upon hearing Nikki's voice. If caught, Will would certainly receive the ribbing of his life.

* * * * *

Nikki and Missy spent Thanksgiving together on the base. They wanted to have a traditional holiday dinner, but neither one wanted to do the cooking. Being an American holiday the club on base was the only alternative. They stuffed themselves with all the turkey, dressing, cranberry sauce, sweet potatoes, and wine they could hold, leaving just enough room for a big piece of pumpkin pie.

"I can't believe we ate all that," Nikki said as she looked over the empty dishes on the table.

"I'm just glad we don't have to wash the dishes," Missy replied as she drank down the last of her wine. "Hey, I have an idea. Why don't you come stay at our house tonight? We can have a good old-fashioned girls' sleepover. You don't need to be driving home anyway with all the wine you've just consumed."

"I'd love to. I guess that's one good thing about being married to a Gunny Sergeant, you get one of the nice houses on the base, huh?"

They walked the few short blocks to Missy and Garrett's house. It was warm and cozy. Missy had a knack for decorating. When you walked in the door, it was like you opened up the pages of a *Southern Living* magazine. Missy liked traditional furnishings with a touch of the eclectic. Only Missy could make them work together so beautifully.

"More wine?" Missy asked Nikki, as she grabbed a bottle from the fridge.

"Why not? As long as you promise not to take advantage of me?" She laughed, as Missy jerked her head up to stare at her.

"You know I can't promise that. My man has been gone too long already. I might need to sway to the other side of the fence."

"I know you too well, Missy. You'll save yourself for Garrett's hot beef injection," Nikki said, as she burst out laughing.

"Nikki Phillips! I have never heard you use such language! I need to get you drunk more often," Missy said as she handed Nikki her glass. "You're a hoot!"

They spent the evening listening to old Motown music, drinking wine and telling stories of their pasts. Nikki told her about Brandon.

"What a fucker!" Missy frowned at Nikki.

"Yea, I know. But, he will have to be fucking someone else because it isn't going to be me," she said clinking her glass to Missy's.

Missy found Nikki a nightshirt and showed her to the guest bedroom. Nikki climbed into bed glancing at the alarm clock that read 3:02 a.m. She smiled thinking how nice it was to have a friend here to share things with. She missed her cousin, Roxie, with whom she'd shared everything since childhood. She missed her parents. Both of them helped her pick herself back up from the devastation after Brandon. But more than all of them, she missed Will.

Closing her eyes she whispered, *I love you, Will.*

* * * * *

Will lay quietly on his cot staring at the bunk above him. *What are you doing tonight?* He thought to himself. He, Gunny, and the other Marines spent Thanksgiving working, intercepting and translating transmissions. Even exhausted, he couldn't sleep. He wanted to hold Nikki so badly. He'd never craved a woman so much in his life. Will rolled over again to stare at the clock. It showed 3:03 a.m.

Chapter Sixteen

As the holidays grew nearer, the Marines grew edgier. All of them longed to be with their loved ones, instead of being packed together like sardines in the tiny barracks. Gunny was the worse for wear. He would spend Christmas with his new bride, and that was all he had to say on the matter. Thankfully, he held just enough rank to pull a few strings.

Gunny walked into the barracks as the men stood at attention. "At ease, men," he told them as he removed his cap. "You Marines have been working hard. Things have quieted down a bit, so our efforts aren't needed for a few days. Besides, my bride will be pissed if she doesn't get any action on Christmas Eve," he said smiling.

"You will all have a three day liberty back to England, and will report back to base on December twenty-sixth at 0800 hours."

"Sir, yes sir," the men said, looking astonished.

Gunny smiled when he walked out of the door hearing his men's cheers of excitement.

✳ ✳ ✳ ✳ ✳

Nikki loved Christmas. She busily decorated her home with decorations she brought over from Texas. The tree was a bit smaller than she preferred, but seemed lovely just the same. Every ornament held some tradition or family story behind it. Decorating for the holidays brightened her spirits a little. The angel on top added the final touch as she sang along with George Strait's version of *Frosty the Snowman* playing in the background.

Her family would be arriving in a few days. Her mother, father, Roxie and Aaron decided to come when they found out Nikki would be alone at Christmas.

"No daughter of mine will be spending the holidays alone," Allison told her.

Nikki anticipated her house being full of people and food. The Phillips family went overboard during the holidays, so there were

94

always plenty of both. She remembered as a child having so many presents to open that a break was needed in the middle of the unwrapping. One year, her mother finished opening the gifts for her.

Nikki's birth was a difficult one for Allison. There were some complications so the doctor performed a hysterectomy. David and Allison focused their whole lives on Nikki, knowing that she would be their only child. They didn't spoil her, but raised her to appreciate the small things in life. They showered her with love, rather than material things. Christmas was their time to be a little frivolous.

David's brother and sister-in-law had a daughter, Roxanne, and a son, Ryan. Nikki adored Roxie. She was the older sister she'd never had. Roxie liked having another girl in the family to discuss her problems with.

Nikki couldn't wait to see her parents, but she wanted to talk to Roxie about Will. She had written letters to her explaining things as they went along, but nothing took the place of a good heart to heart with your best girlfriend. Nikki would miss Will terribly. In fact, if her family wasn't coming to see her, she probably would have blown the holiday off all together this year. The idea of spending such a glorious holiday alone never bothered her before. However, Will was not a major part of her life before. How and when did she become so utterly wrapped up in this man? Hmmm, probably the first time she ever laid eyes on him in the Joiner Arms.

Chapter Seventeen

"Daddy!" Nikki yelled as her father came off the train. She ran to him throwing her arms around his neck and kissing him hard on the cheek.

"How's my girl?"

"Glad that y'all are here," she said grabbing her mother to hug them both.

"England's been good to you, I see," her mother told her, pinching her cheek.

Roxie came off the train with Aaron in her arms. She joined Allison and Nikki in a tight hug. Aaron squealed with delight as his family pulled him into the center of the circle. Nikki kissed him on the forehead.

"It's so good to see y'all again. I didn't know how much I missed you until I saw you get off that train," Nikki said as she grabbed two of the suitcases. "We'll have to grab a cab. I took one in to town because I knew we wouldn't all be able to fit in my car."

With the luggage and Aaron's car seat, it took two cabs to get back to Nikki's house. She put her parents in her room, and Roxie and Aaron in the spare bedroom. Nikki would sleep on the sofa during their visit. They settled in the living room, while Nikki made a pot of tea.

"Your house is simply lovely, Nikki. You always liked to go all out for the holidays," Allison said admiring Nikki's Christmas tree.

"Gee, I wonder where I got that from?" she asked facetiously.

"Are you still watching *Eastenders*?" Allison asked her.

"I never miss it. I taped several episodes for you. I knew that you were having withdrawal from your stories. That show and reruns of *Dallas* have helped me pass the time since Will has been gone."

"It's nice to know that you still think about your mum every now and then. I thought that this new man in your life had made you forget about your family," she said smiling over her cup.

"When is your Marine going to be back so we can meet him?" asked David.

"He won't be back until sometime in May."

"Well, he's a good Marine or they wouldn't have sent him there. I look forward to it." David sipped his tea with a serious look on his face.

The next day was Christmas Eve. Roxie needed to pick up a few more stocking stuffers for Aaron so she and Nikki hit the shops. Nikki bought a box of chocolate delicacies for her mother, who she knew adored them. She picked up some of her father's favorite cigars and they turned back toward the cottage. They stopped for tea and rum truffles before heading back home.

The Marines arrived in London early that afternoon. Before getting on the north-bound train, Will wanted to make a stop first. He walked into the first jewelry store he came across. He wasn't quite sure what to buy, but felt that the perfect piece would jump out at him. He was right. In the last glass showcase he looked in, he found a beautiful opal heart pendant. He envisioned reflecting her eyes making them all the more beautiful. He could picture it hanging above her creamy breasts. The thought made his stomach flutter.

Allison cooked most of the day. Nikki loved her mother's Yorkshire pudding, and Roxie told her no chef could make a trifle like she did. It pleased her to have a crowd to cook for.

She'd put herself and David on a fat-free, low sugar, low carbohydrate diet for the last few weeks. The holidays were a time for splurging, and she intended to do so during her visit to her homeland. They could get back on a strict regimen when they returned to the states.

Allison finished setting the table when Roxie and Nikki returned. Aaron ran to his mother holding his arms up to be picked up.

"Hey, baby boy. Did you have fun with Unk today?" She lifted Aaron up and kissed him on the cheek.

"Do you have a kiss for your cousin, Aaron?" Nikki kissed him on the forehead leaving a deep red lip mark. They walked into the den and found David, snoring on the sofa with the newspaper over his face.

"I'm afraid Aaron wore out the old *Pooh*," Allison said as she entered the room, wiping her hands on a dishtowel.

"Did you make Yorkshire pudding?" Nikki asked sniffing the aroma filling the house.

"That I did, and your favorite meat pies. And, trifle for Roxie."

"I didn't think we were going to have a big meal until tomorrow night?" Nikki asked her mother as she kissed her on the cheek.

"We bloody well have to eat tonight, don't we? I never get to cook good food anymore. I just had to get started early."

"Well, good. Then you definitely deserve the surprise I brought you," she said, as she pulled out the recognizable box.

"My dear child, rum truffles?" she asked knowingly.

"Of course."

David stumbled into the kitchen sleepy eyed. "Do I smell food?"

"That you do, my love. Why don't you sit yourself at the table while we get things prepared in here."

David took Aaron with him and set him in his highchair. The girls entered and put the serving dishes along the buffet.

"Everything looks mighty tasty," David said as he patted Allison on the behind. "You haven't cooked like this in a while. I think I forgot what butter tastes like," he said, as he dabbed some on the Yorkshire pudding he held in his hand.

Everyone ate heartily. Aaron enjoyed playing with his food more so than eating it, so bits and pieces circled around the legs of his highchair. Nikki refilled everyone's glasses with wine and cleared the dishes from the table.

"Momma, you and Daddy go relax in the den. I'll do the dishes," Nikki told her parents as she rolled up the sleeves of her silk blouse. Roxie went upstairs to give Aaron a bath and put him to bed. Nikki sang Christmas carols as she scraped a baking pan. The running water and her voice were loud enough to drown out the sound of the doorbell.

Chapter Eighteen

When Nikki didn't stop singing, David got up to answer the door. Will stood on the stoop with his duffel bag slung over his shoulder. He headed straight to Nikki's when he got off the train. Will looked tired and nervous; David thought when he opened the door.

"It's about time you got here, Marine. I'm David Phillips, Nikki's dad. You must be Will."

"It's a pleasure to meet you, sir," he said as he extended his hand to David.

Good, firm handshake, David thought to himself. He put his finger over his mouth motioning Will to enter quietly. Will followed him to the kitchen. His heart jumped in his throat when he saw her standing over the sink. David walked back into the den shutting the French doors behind him. Will smiled as he listened to her quietly singing *Silent Night.* He came up behind her and gently kissed the back of her neck. She startled and turned quickly, putting her hand to her mouth to muffle her squeal of surprise.

"Will! What are—? How did—? I can't believe you're here," she said as she flung her arms around his neck and kissed him hard.

"Gunny didn't want to spend Christmas without Missy, so he got us all a three day liberty. I have to go back the day after tomorrow."

"Well, I have you for two days. That's more than I expected. God, it is so good to see you."

"I have missed you more than you could ever know," he told her as he held her close to him.

"Good grief," exclaimed Roxie as she entered the kitchen. "I was only upstairs for forty-five minutes and you already found yourself another man?"

"No, Roxie. This is Will. He got to come back for Christmas. Can you believe it? Will, this is my cousin, Roxanne McNamara."

"Will, I am very glad to meet you. You have turned my little cousin's life upside down, I hope you know," she said smiling at the handsome Marine in his fatigues. "You are just as gorgeous as she said you were."

"You'll have to excuse my cousin, Will. She doesn't always know when to keep her big mouth shut," Nikki said as she punched her softly in the arm.

"Would you like to come and meet my parents?"

"Your dad answered the door."

"Was he nice or do I need to go and punch him, too?"

"He's a fellow jarhead, Nikki. I reckon we'll get along fine."

Nikki opened the doors to the den. David had already filled Allison in on what had happened.

"Will, I am so glad that you could join us for the holiday," Allison said as she warmly took his hands in hers and squeezed gently.

"It's my pleasure, Mrs. Phillips."

"Oh, we'll have none of that bloody formality. Call me Allison."

"Yes, ma'am... I mean, Allison."

Nikki poured Will a glass of wine and the five of them sat in the den to visit. Will fit in perfectly with her family. He and David talked about the Corps while the three women chattered and smiled approvingly at the two of them. An hour later, Allison stood up and said, "Well love, we should be getting to bed. You know Aaron will be up early to see what Father Christmas brought him." She grabbed David's hand and led him upstairs.

"You two don't do anything I wouldn't do," said Roxie smiling slyly as she followed David and Allison upstairs.

Nikki grabbed Will's collar and pulled him to her. "I just want to smell you. Maybe then I will believe that you're actually here."

Will kissed her deeply sliding his hand up the back of her neck and through her hair. Their tongues reacquainted themselves as he pulled her into him harder. He immediately could feel the tightening of his loins as they continued their passionate embrace.

"I feel like I'm in high school again, with your parents right upstairs," he told her, as he kissed around her face.

"Yea, but I'm a grownup, so what are they going to do, ground me?"

"I don't know. But, I'm sure your dad could lay me out if he wanted to."

"Daddy likes you. I can tell."

"That might change if he came down and found my hands all over his little girl."

Nikki kissed him softly on his eyelids and on each cheekbone. She couldn't believe he was actually home.

"It's late, Nikki, and I'm tired. I'd better get home."

"I want you to stay with me."

"You know I couldn't disrespect your parents that way. I would be on pins and needles the whole night if I stayed here. I want your dad to know that I respect you and them."

"It's my house, Will. I'm not a teenager anymore."

"I know that. Just be patient. We'll have time together when it's right. I don't want to leave either, but I feel that it's the right thing to do."

"Okay, but you had better come back over here first thing in the morning. Aaron will be up early so don't dilly dally," she said kissing him deeply before he walked down the steps.

"I love you, Nikki. I'll be here, first light." He walked quickly home in the brisk night air.

Nikki tossed and turned on the sofa. She couldn't stop thinking how much she wanted Will to make love to her. The mantle clock chimed one o'clock. She got up and looked out the window towards Will's house. His lights were on. That was all the invitation she needed. She went to the downstairs bathroom and took off her clothes. She made sure she looked somewhat presentable and then wrapped her coat around her. She opened the front door quietly and scurried to his house.

When Will opened the door he already had a smirk on his face.

"Look, I can't take this," Nikki told him. "I can't sleep and I know you can't either. Let me in, and screw my brains out," she said as she opened her coat to him.

"Oh, God, Nikki. I hoped you'd see my light on." He grabbed her then and pulled her into his arms. She could feel him harden against her as they kissed passionately in the doorway. He shut the door and pushed her back into it abruptly.

Will ripped her coat from her body, letting it fall to the floor. Grabbing her hand, he all but dragged her to the den laying her down on the sofa. He tore at his clothes not getting them off quickly enough.

Nikki lay seductively on the sofa admiring his body. He knelt down to the side of the sofa and ran his hands over her silky smooth body.

"God, I've missed you," he said as he kissed one breast and then the other.

"I can't stand one more minute without feeling you, Will."

"You don't have to wait anymore. I'm all yours," he told her between kisses.

The sweat began to trickle down his back as the heat between them intensified. His mouth made a trail from her breasts to the top of the coarse curls that covered her, and then down the inside of her thighs. Nikki relished the incredible sensation generated by his tongue. On the return journey to her mouth, Nikki couldn't hold back the squeal that escaped her throat.

"Will, God, you make me feel like I'm going to explode."

"Oh, Darlin', that's not even close to how you make me feel."

He teased her senses by dipping his thick shaft inside her beckoning pussy, and then pulling himself out gently, again and again.

"God, Will, take me now. I want to feel your dick inside me. Please," she begged, as her body pulsed with desire for him.

He thrust his hard cock into her, fully and completely. Plunging in between her legs made her squeal with delight. Their bodies meshed together as they peaked in unison, fully and uncontrollably. For the first time in his life, he couldn't hold back the emotion he felt for her. He moaned loudly as he filled her. She answered him with a high moan of her own. They held each other tightly until the throbbing of his cock eased inside her.

They lay together sleeping for hours before Nikki awoke. She quietly put on her coat to go back home. Looking down at Will, her heart sank in her chest at the sight of his peacefulness.

She'd never loved anyone as much as she did him. Just looking at him made her tingle all over.

Nikki tiptoed down the hall and out the door then ran quickly to her house. The sun was just beginning to peek over the horizon when she opened her front door to her father awaiting her arrival.

"Uh...Hi, Daddy," she said blushing.

"Well, did you enjoy your evening?"

"Daddy, you weren't supposed to be up yet." She bit her lip and felt like a schoolgirl who got caught sneaking out at night. *Well, let's face it. You did sneak out last night,* she thought to herself.

"Once a Marine, always a Marine. I can't sleep past dawn. I know what you two were up to. I can't say that your mother and I didn't have times we couldn't keep our hands off of each other."

"Okay, Daddy... TMI."

"What in the hell is TMI?"

"Too much information!" She smiled at him as he took her in his big arms and squeezed tight.

"You're not a little girl anymore, Nikki. I can't say that I like knowing what you were doing over there, but I can't stop you now can I? Do you love this boy?"

"Yes, Daddy, I do. I just haven't told him though."

"Does he love you? Never mind. I can see for myself that the boy is plum crazy over you."

"He is, and I feel so blessed to have him love me so much."

"Then, you need to tell the boy that. Nothing's worse then being kept hanging. We'll just let this be our little secret. Your mother doesn't need to know every little detail," he smiled down at her and kissed the top of her head, just like he did when she was little. "How about some coffee?"

"I love you, Daddy."

"I love you most."

Chapter Nineteen

Will bolted up when he realized that she no longer remained. He ran upstairs to shower, shave, and dress before going to Nikki's. He wondered if her family knew about last night. He hoped they didn't, especially her father.

Will wore a denim, long-sleeved shirt over his white t-shirt. He tucked it into his favorite jeans and then slid on his boots. He added his belt and watch. Looking in the mirror, he pulled at the bags under his eyes with his fingers. His bloodshot eyes stared back at him. He didn't get near enough sleep. Oh well, they would have to like him the way he was. He dabbed on a bit of cologne and headed out the door, grabbing his jacket and the small wrapped box on his way.

Will knocked quietly, just in case her family still slept. He expected her cousin, Aaron, was up to see what Santa brought him. He felt his stomach turn over when David answered the door.

"You're here awful early, Marine," David said not smiling.

"Nikki told me to be here first thing, so here I am, sir."

"Why don't you come on in? Nikki's in the shower and the rest of them are still sleeping," he smiled then, remembering the first time he met Allison's parents and the nerves shooting through his body. He would give the poor guy a bit of a break, maybe.

"Thank you, sir." Will stepped in cautiously and followed David to the kitchen.

"Coffee?"

"Yes, sir. Thank you, sir," Will said wiping his palms on the front of his pants.

"You can call me David."

"David, my name's Will."

"Point taken," David slapped him on the back as they drank their coffee in a more relaxed state. They were laughing when Nikki walked in.

"What are you two up to in here?" Nikki asked as she poured herself a cup of coffee.

"Nothing," Will said quickly before David could open his mouth.

"That's a scary thought."

"Just don't you worry your pretty little head about it," Will said as he kissed her on the cheek and put his arm around her waist.

"Good morning, love," Allison said, entering the kitchen and smiling at her husband of twenty-five years.

David set his cup on the counter and turned around to face her. He covered her mouth with his and kissed her passionately. Nikki and Will stood watching them and then looked at each other in amazement.

"Crikey! Have you gone bloody mad? What on earth has come over you, David? And, in front of the children."

"Let's just say it's for making me happy all these years."

Nikki thought she'd cry. Her parents demonstrated their commitment without saying a word. They held hands when taking her to the park as a child. They kissed each other lovingly every morning before David left for work. And 'I love you' was spoken several times during the day by all of them. Nikki lived a wonderful life. She hoped someday, her children would look to her and Will with the same adoration she looked at her parents with this day, in her kitchen. With Will…their children. That had a wonderful ring to it.

"Sanna Cause!" Aaron screamed as he ran down the stairs with his mother on his heels.

Roxie caught him just before he tumbled all the way down. "Calm down, son. You don't want to break your neck before you get to open your presents, now do you?"

She scooped him up and carried him into the kitchen with the others. "I think someone is ready to see what Santa brought him."

"You think?" Nikki said teasingly.

They all meandered into the den as Roxie tried to calm Aaron down before he tore into every present under the tree. Nikki played Santa's helper, complete with elf hat, and stacked everyone's gifts in front of them. The adults waited patiently while Aaron opened all of his. Christmas was even more special when seen through the eyes of a child. Aaron tore through the paper with hurried excitement as he opened a fighter plane, several toy dumptrucks, coloring books and crayons, candy canes, and a baseball cap.

"That's a book about Postman Pat and his black and white cat, Jesse. It's a favorite with the children over here," Nikki said as she helped him unwrap her gift. "Postman Pat. Postman Pat. Postman Pat and his black and white cat," Nikki sang the theme song from Saturday morning cartoons. Maybe no one would figure out that she watched cartoons on Saturdays.

"And how would you know how that little ditty goes?" Will asked her smiling.

Busted, Nikki thought to herself. She bit her lip in embarrassment as she changed the subject quickly. Will was charmed.

"This is for you, Daddy," Nikki said, handing her father the box of cigars she had purchased the day before.

"See, Ally, my little girl does love me after all," he said, as he kissed the top of her head.

"And this one's for you, Roxie."

Roxie opened the box carefully. "A teapot! Oh, how lovely! Thank you so much, Nikki," she said kissing her on the cheek.

"Okay, Momma, open yours."

"Nikki, it's gorgeous. Simply gorgeous. I have always wanted this one, too," she said, opening the box of a cottage to go with her collection at home.

Nikki felt nervous. She hoped Will would like her gift. She'd found the perfect gift for him when she and Roxie went shopping yesterday. Something pulled at her heart to buy it and hold on to it. She was so glad she did.

"This one's for you, Will," she said shyly as she handed him the package.

"Nikki, I wasn't expecting anything."

"All the more reason to get something, don't you think?"

The only sound in the room was that of the crinkling of paper. Will removed the music box and recognized it as Prince Charming kissing Cinderella.

"It's for being my Prince Charming."

"I love it, Nikki. I'll keep it with me all the time." He kissed her softly on the mouth, almost taking more before realizing that her family stared at them.

"Uh, hum." Will cleared his throat, and decided that it was now or never. "Nikki, I have something for you, too."

He handed her the small box, in red paper with gold wire ribbon. Her fingers shook as she carefully pulled the ribbon and paper off the long velvet box. She could feel the heat move up her chest as she opened it.

"Oh, Will. It's beautiful," she said as she held the opal across her chest.

Just as he expected, it fell just between the tops of her breasts. "It looked like you," Will said. "I could see the color of your eyes in it."

"She does have some killer eyes doesn't she?" Roxie said, with a tinge of jealousy to her tone. "I've always hated her for that!"

✳ ✳ ✳ ✳ ✳

The afternoon was spent with lots of food, laughs, and spirits. David brought out his traditional bottle of bourbon, and poured him and Will a jigger full. They drank it down and then both enjoyed a cigar. Nikki could hardly contain the joy bursting out of her. She knew she had fallen for him, hook, line and sinker. She loved seeing him with her father, the men she loved more than life itself, enjoying each other's company.

"I'm going to stay at Will's tonight, Momma," she said as the three women drank tea at the dining table.

Allison looked up at her daughter. "I wouldn't have thought otherwise, my darling. I would do the same if it was your father's last night home before going away for months."

"Yeah, get it while you can," Roxie said as she giggled in her cup.

"And here I was fretting over the idea you two would think I was a slut for going to a man's bed before marriage," Nikki said.

They all smiled and finished their tea as the men entered the room. Nikki went upstairs to pack an overnight bag to take to Will's. As she pulled clothes from the armoire, she stopped suddenly to stare at the pendant around her neck. It was gorgeous. She didn't deserve to be this happy.

"Are you ready?" Will's deep voice jerked her back to reality.

"Almost," she said as she threw the last few items in her bag.

"I love you, Spunky. You know that don't you?"

"I do know that. I am working on believing it."

He held her tight, and they turned to go downstairs.

✳ ✳ ✳ ✳ ✳

As Christmas day proved the best day of her life, the day after proved one of her worst. She dreaded Will leaving her again.

Will packed his things in silence, avoiding the tension between them. He wasn't so sure his voice wouldn't crack if he had to speak. He'd carried out departures a dozen times and more. But, leaving the woman he loved desperately, tore him up inside. He spied the tears in her eyes each time they met his.

Last night had been rendered magical. They had loved each other more tenderly than before. It had almost been as if she finally loved him as much as he loved her. However, it hurt knowing she couldn't say the words he so desperately needed to hear.

Nikki fought back the tears as she drove Will to the base. She held on tightly to the steering wheel, trying not to lose control in front of him. The heat from Will's hand resting on her thigh radiated through her. As they pulled into the base he squeezed it gently. Nikki felt nauseated as they stepped out of the car to say their good-byes.

"I'll be back before you know it."

Nikki continued to look down at his boots. "It seems like a lifetime away, Will."

He took her chin in his hand and raised her face so their eyes met. "I love you. Don't ever forget that. Remember—Semper Fi."

"Always faithful," Nikki said as the tears began to well from her eyes and pour down her cheeks.

He grabbed her and kissed her hard until he finally had to pull himself away.

"I'll call you Sunday, okay?"

"Okay."

He kissed her once again and then turned to walk toward the rest of the regiment waiting for him. Nikki got in her car and sobbed with her face in her hands, as she heard the military vehicle drive past her. *God, I love him.*

Chapter Twenty

David, Allison and Roxie stayed another week after Christmas. This being Roxie's first trip to England, David and Allison took her to see all the sights. In the afternoons, when Nikki got home from work, she and Roxie found a footpath and took long walks together. They often found themselves trekking through someone's cow pasture or backyard. Roxie became increasingly fascinated with this land so new to her.

"What would I have to do to find a teaching job on the base?"

"I'm not sure. Are you thinking about moving here?" Nikki stared at Roxie intently.

"I think I could be happy here, Nikki. This would be such a great place to raise Aaron."

"I would love to have you two here! We'll go to the base tomorrow and see what kind of red tape you have to go through."

Roxie decided quickly England was the place she wanted to raise her son. The base administrator gave her all the paperwork necessary to obtain her government clearance to teach there.

Roxie fumbled through the monotonous waste of trees while on the airplane back to Texas. Aaron slept soundly, so she relaxed and dreamt of a successful life for herself and her son.

✳ ✳ ✳ ✳ ✳

Nikki left work early on a Friday, two weeks later, and hopped on a plane to Germany. She wanted to surprise Will.

When she got to her hotel room, she called the pager number Will had given her. Nikki left her cell phone number for him to call her back. Within minutes, he called sounding distressed.

"What is it? Are you okay?"

"I'm fine. I just didn't want you to know where I was. I have a little surprise up my sleeve."

"You do? And what kind of surprise might that be?"

"It's classified. If I told you, I'd have to kill you."

He could feel her smile over the phone. "I have a clearance, you know?"

"I'll give you clearance, baby. Why don't you meet me at Neu Heidelberg? That is, if you don't have any other plans." The sweat began to bead across her upper lip, as she became excited about where this phone call was leading. "I have some very nasty things that I want to do to you."

"Hell, I'd go AWOL if that's the only way I could get to you." Will could feel his pants begin to tighten through his groin.

"Nothing that drastic. Just get your sexy, tight ass to the hotel. I'm in room thirty-eight. I'll leave the door unlocked. Oh, yeah, leave your underwear in the barracks. You won't be needing them." She hung up the phone and quickly got everything ready for a night of seduction.

Will walked into her room and tried to focus his eyes in the candlelight. He couldn't find Nikki, at first, but as he walked through to the bed, there she lay. She'd spread herself across the bed in a racy, red silk chemise. Her dark black hair was pulled up high off her shoulders in the style that he liked best. Candles glistened all over the room. Nikki brought champagne that now chilled in a bucket next to two glasses on the nightstand. He'd swear her eyes glowed by the light of the candles. They beckoned him to come closer. He obeyed.

"What have you got on underneath that coat, Will?"

"Just enough so I wouldn't freeze on the way over here. My damn dick was so hard when I hung up the phone I didn't think I'd ever get my skivvies on!"

Nikki flung her head back and laughed hard at his comment. "I love it when you talk dirty, Will," she said seductively once she gained her composure.

He slid on the bed next to her, letting his hands rub up and down the smooth satin on her back. His fully erect cock pressed against her thighs as it poked out of his boxers.

"I couldn't stay away from you," she said as she started unbuttoning his shirt. Her hands slowly rubbed through the thick hair on his chest and over his shoulders.

"I'm glad you came. It's been a long week. I needed this."

"Well, let's just relieve all the stress now, okay?" Nikki continued to run her hands over his skin. Her fingers traced the treasure trail from his navel to his bulging cock. She grabbed hold of it and stroked it firmly, but gently as his juices oozed from the excitement.

"Oh, baby. You have such talented fingers," he whispered to her as he lifted her breasts from the top of the chemise. He fondled them, feeling her aroused nipples taut with want. Nikki slid his boxers all the way down as she curled into him.

He closed his eyes and enjoyed the massaging of her fingers. She pushed his shirt off leaving his chest bare, beckoning her. Nikki ran her hands over his hardened nipples, down his sides, and up his back. She kissed the hollow in his chest as she continued to rub her hands over his arms.

"You know this is my favorite part of your body. I love the feel of those little hairs through my fingers, in that dip in the center of your chest."

She guided his stiff cock through the dark, curly patch between her legs to the small pucker of skin that pulsated with need. She rubbed him on her nub as he moaned with need. He soon loosened his cock from her grip and held her hands over her head. He removed the chemise from her silky skin, kissing her as it left her body.

"Fuck me, Will. Just fuck my brains out. I want it hard, fast, and now!"

"You are a bad girl tonight, aren't you?" He pulled her close to him, as he plunged into her slick pussy. He dove into her deeper, banging her head against the wall.

"Damn it. I'm sorry, Nikki."

"Don't stop, Will. I'm okay. Come with me. Now!" she groaned to him in ecstasy.

Nikki squeaked as the release of orgasm shot through her. Will's heaving cock pulsed inside her slippery pussy as he poured his hot seed into every inch of her body.

"I could go for some squirt cheese about now," Nikki laughed.

"Even though I hate to admit it, that does sound kind of good."

They lay together in the afterglow, silently. Nikki smiled dreamily as she ran her fingers down his arms. Will contemplated the best way to tell her his news. It wasn't going to be easy.

✳ ✳ ✳ ✳ ✳

The next morning as they dressed, they ordered breakfast in the room.

"I have some news, Nikki. I'm going back to the states."

"What?"

"I've finally been accepted to Officer Candidate School. I'll be going to Virginia on March first. I want you to come with me. I can't stand being away from you anymore."

"Damn it! I thought you were going to be in England for another year at least."

"We can get married. Then, you can come back with me as Mrs. Chambers."

"You don't get it do you? What am I going to do about my job? I am under a contract, you know?"

"Your contract can be—"

"I'll never be able to hold a job again. You realize that if I'm a Marine's wife, basically I'll never have any kind of a career." Nikki could feel the heat spread up her throat. It angered her that he would have her uproot herself from a life she'd built on her own, to follow him, wherever he went.

"I can't believe you are making such a big deal out of this, Nikki." Will was beginning to get angry with her as well. How could she not want to come with him? He knew she loved him, even though she had never actually said it. "I don't have a choice. I have to go wherever the Corps sends me. Unless, you would like to be the breadwinner in the family."

"And what would be so wrong with that?" Nikki realized they had never talked about her career. Will expected her to go with him. She never considered the resentment it would cause. "My job's important to me, Will. This is the first time I have been on my own completely. Don't you realize it's important to me? Why do you want to take away my independence?"

"I'm not taking away your independence, Nikki. I guess we should have discussed this before. Being a Marine is my life. It's more than just a job. It's who I am, and who I will be, until the day I die."

Nikki fumed, as she paced the floor of the hotel. "That's all fine and dandy, but what about who I am? Doesn't that matter to you?"

"Shit, Nikki, I didn't think I would have to go through this with you."

"What do you mean? You just thought I would burn all my bridges and follow you like a lost puppy?"

"You are acting like a spoiled bitch," he muttered as he pulled on his boots.

"What in the hell did you just say?" Nikki stared at him in a rage he had never seen in her before.

"I said you are acting like a spoiled bitch!"

Before Nikki could stop herself she slapped Will across the face. "How dare you call me that! Why don't you just get out! I don't want to look at you!"

Will clenched his fist to control himself from swinging back at her. "Fine. We'll talk about this again, once you have control of yourself." He put his jacket on and slammed the door behind him.

Nikki felt sick. Why couldn't he understand how she felt? Where in the hell did he get off calling her that? She knew she could be a bitch from time to time. But, that didn't give him the right to say it. He's lucky I only slapped him and didn't kick him in the balls! Well, we will just see about that, Will Chambers. I am not going to be your doormat!

Chapter Twenty-One

Will grew more pissed each day when he called and she didn't answer. She couldn't avoid him forever. He would finish this conversation with her if it was the last thing he did!

Nikki spent the next two weeks buried in her work. She barked at her fellow workers and avoided her friends. She was miserable, but she was not going to give in to him. Will had called her the past two Sundays, but she refused to answer the phone. She wasn't ready to talk to him, yet. Marines don't budge an inch and she knew that. Nikki remembered several arguments her parents had while she was growing up and how her mother would finally give in. Nikki was not going to give in!

"You want to tell me what's eating you?" Phil came in her office and closed the door.

"Not really," she said not turning away from her computer.

"Let's put it this way. You either tell me or I'm suspending you."

"Look, Phil, I know you mean well. But, I'll deal with it on my own."

"Obviously you can't deal with it on your own and that's why you are snapping at everyone around you." Phil sat down on the corner of her desk and drank from his coffee cup. "Missy said she hasn't talked to you in weeks. I thought you would talk to her if anybody. Does this have to do with Will?"

"Of course," Nikki said leaning back in her chair. "Who else could piss me off so much that it interrupts my whole life?"

Nikki drank down the cold coffee that remained in her cup. She winced as she swallowed it and then looked up at Phil. "Are you sure you want to hear this?"

"Hit me," Phil said to her smiling.

"Will is being transferred back to the states in March. He wants us to get married, and me to move there with him. I told him that I am under contract here, but he doesn't seem to care about my obligations.

He is being a real asshole about the whole thing, Phil. I know he has to go, but I love my job. That doesn't seem to matter to him."

"Maybe he knows that your job isn't the problem."

"What is that supposed to mean?" Nikki looked puzzled.

"Where in the states is he headed?"

"Quantico, Officer Candidate School."

"You know we have branches all over the United States. It would be easy enough to have you complete your contract over there."

Nikki's eyes became big and round with astonishment. "You mean I wouldn't have to lose my government clearance?"

"Hell, no. Is that what has been eating at you for the past two weeks? Damn, Nikki, all you had to do was come and talk to me. You're a very talented young woman. I wouldn't let your expertise go to waste."

"Oh, God, Phil. I have really screwed up! I have to call Will. I have to tell him that I'm an idiot. Can you see what you can find out for me about transferring?"

"You betcha. You go and get your man back."

Nikki ran out of the office faster than lightning. She had a lot of sucking up to do.

Chapter Twenty-Two

"Where in the hell are you, Will?" Nikki asked as she paged him for the third time. She finally called the number he gave her for emergencies. A clerk answered the phone and told her that Will was on liberty and there was no way to get in touch with him. Nikki cursed as she slammed the receiver back down on the phone. He must be really pissed if he took leave without telling her.

✻ ✻ ✻ ✻ ✻

Will was sick and tired of playing these stupid little games. He wasn't going to take the silent treatment anymore. He didn't care what happened, but they were going to have it out, and have it out now! The cab pulled into her driveway. He ran up to the door, but she didn't answer.

"Damn it, Nikki. Where in the hell are you?"

He walked to his house and got into his jeep. *Maybe she was working late*, he thought. He headed for the base.

The rage began to overtake him when he saw her car parked in front of the bar. How could she party while he'd been stewing in misery for the past few weeks?

"Freaking women!" He slammed the door on his jeep and headed inside.

Missy excused herself to the ladies' room. Nikki was surrounded by several guys who were friends of Missy's when Will walked in. She threw her head back in laughter at one of the men's jokes before being grabbed firmly on the arm. She stopped laughing suddenly and looked up into Will's angry eyes.

"Excuse us," Will said as he dragged her away from the bar.

"Will, let go of me!"

"No way. I am sick and tired of this shit! What in the hell were you doing in there? Trying to pick up some other sucker?"

"How dare you! You don't own me, Will Chambers!" Nikki jerked her arm from his grip and they stood together staring at each other furiously.

Before they knew it, the magnetic force of their love pulled them together in a passionate embrace. Their teeth clinked together briefly as he took her mouth with his.

Missy flew out of the bar door to see where Nikki disappeared to. She stood smiling as she saw them in each other's arms.

Way to go, Will, she said to herself and turned to go back inside.

Will and Nikki stood gasping for air when they finally broke away from each other. Their anger disappeared, leaving only forgiveness.

"I couldn't take it anymore, Nikki. I can't stand to be without you."

"What? Is that where you've been? I've been trying to call you for days."

"Yeah, I took some leave because there were some things that needed to be done. I can't believe you've made me so damn weak!"

"You're not weak, Will. You're just in love with me as much as I am with you. We both have been stupid and hardheaded." She paused a moment and kicked the dirt with her shoe.

"I talked to Phil. He said there was an engineering branch at the base in Quantico. I could transfer, but that's not what I'm going to do. I want you to go to Officer Candidate School and become an Officer. I don't want to be a distraction. I'll be here when you come back in six months, waiting for you."

"Did you really say that you loved me?" Will asked her trying to capture her gaze with his eyes.

"I did. I do, I just haven't been able to get beyond my fears to tell you. I need to share all of myself with you, always."

"God, do you know how long I have wanted to hear you say that?"

"Oh, Will. I think I've loved you since the first time I ran into you. I've been a fool not to tell you before now," Nikki said to him as she ran her fingers across his cheek.

"I was hoping that you would finally cave," he said gratefully. "I had already done some checking on your job before I talked to you that night. I didn't get to tell you before you slugged me."

"I'm really sorry about that. I don't think you'll be calling me that again anytime soon, huh?"

"Not unless I'm an idiot."

They both laughed as she fell into him. He felt so warm and comforting. She couldn't believe what a bitch she had been to him.

"Well, I guess we survived our first fight," she said to him, laying her head on his chest.

"I reckon that's the second one, isn't it?"

"Oh yea, I forgot."

He kissed her and led her to her car.

"Let's go home. I don't have to be back for a couple of days. We have a lot of making up to do."

* * * * *

She looked up at him and smiled bravely as she turned off the porch light and led him upstairs. Nikki wanted to pleasure him in a way she'd never done for any man. She wanted to give him back all the joy he'd made her feel that first night together.

Nikki continued stroking him softly as he lay across the bed. She ran her fingers down his belly. Her fingers began to slowly unzip his zipper and slide his jeans down to the floor. His cock hardened with each one of her caresses. She carefully removed the boxers to the floor.

Standing over him, she seductively disrobed herself, piece by piece. He stared in amazement as Nikki dropped to her knees and kissed him softly, up the inside of each thigh. Her tongue glided up the path, to the dark patch under his bulging shaft and then massaged each mound as he arched in ecstasy.

Will closed his eyes, as his mind swam with the visions of her loving him. His body tingled when she took his thick cock into her mouth. The warmth and wetness made him shudder. He knew he couldn't hold back the wave of excitement much longer. His heart pounded as he flooded into her. She squeezed the furry mounds firmly, as he continued to convulse with satisfaction.

Will's legs trembled as he lay in the afterglow. Nikki laid her head on his chest and listened to the slowing of his heartbeat.

"God, Nikki. That was incredible."

"I wanted to make you feel what you have given to me."

He kissed the top of her head as she snuggled up next to him. Moments later she could feel him stiffen with desire.

"Are you up for another round?" She asked him as she gently rubbed him with her fingers.

"It's payback time." He rolled her onto her back and began to suck on her nipples. Each flick of his tongue made her throb with desire, as the slickness her cunt made prepared her for him. Nikki rubbed against his cock, feeling the pain of desire surge through her body. She climaxed, pushing him against her.

Slowly, he slid his hard body down her length. His tongue trailed inside her thighs to the hot wetness, hiding beneath the coarse, curly, hairs of her cunt.

The heat from his tongue made her flinch with pleasure as it continued to massage the soft, supple walls protecting her pussy. Her heat rose like lightning as his tongue moved faster and faster. The force of her climax caused her hips to rear up; her legs began to shake, quivering in ecstasy. Will squeezed her buttocks tightly as she continued to writhe in the excruciating pleasure.

Traveling slowly to satisfy her needs, he made his way to her breasts. Grasping her nipples with his teeth, he carefully tugged them slightly, one after the other. She gasped, as the thrill of his mouth coursed through her body. She could feel his hot cock tickling the skin, from her pussy to navel. Her body writhed, pressing his erection into her flesh. Will moaned with pleasure, as he rubbed his cock along her silky skin.

Will entered her, thrusting slowly, as he watched her expressions of pleasure. Her hips danced with his movements, forcing his shaft deeper into her core. His thrusts quickened. Nikki felt the muscles of his ass tighten with each movement. She ran her hands over the tight muscles, up to the ripples along his back. Will's breath quickened. She could feel his dick become firmer with each thrust, knowing he was about to explode.

With a quaking shudder, Will filled her with his liquid passion. She held him tightly as he continued to pour into her. As his cock went deeper into her cunt, she came again. He pulled his dripping cock from her wet pussy and lay with her. She nestled in the crook of his arm. She wrapped them with the blanket, and they slept.

* * * * *

Nikki watched in fear as Will tossed and turned in bed. The sheets around his body were drenched from his profuse sweating. Nikki reached out to comfort him, and wake him from the nightmare.

Will shook his head and stared at Nikki with hazy eyes.

"I'm sorry I woke you up," he said as he flung his legs over the side of the bed.

Nikki was not going to let him shut her out this time. She sat behind him on the bed, and threaded her arms through his, pulling him into her.

Before she could ask him to tell her, he began describing the horrid details.

"I never knew that you could actually smell in your dreams, but I can, Nikki. I can smell the burning flesh of men, women and kids, Nikki. God, it's the kids that tear me up. Body parts were lying all over the desert. Some half buried, some not at all. I try so hard to push it out of my mind, but it won't go away."

"It's who you are now, Will. Just like my past makes me who I am. I'm embarrassed to even compare myself to you, Will. You have lived through a hell of lot worse than I could ever imagine. I just let a jerk rule my life for too long."

"I wanted you to know what's wrong with me," he said as he wiped the tears that escaped from her eyes.

"There's nothing wrong with you, Will. I can't imagine facing the things you have faced and coming out unscathed. We can deal with the nightmares. Let me comfort you. I want to make them go away."

"I don't know if you can, Darlin'. They've been hanging around for a long time now."

"Maybe you just needed the right woman to take away the pain," she said as she held his chin in her hands. "I love you more than anything, Will. Nothing will chase me away. We will deal with this together."

"I was hoping you'd say that. Wait right here," he said as he jumped up from the bed and took something out of the pocket of his jacket.

Gently, he handed her a small black velvet box. Tears formed in her eyes as she held the box in her trembling hands. Will took the ring out of its holder and placed it on her finger. It was the most beautiful diamond she had ever seen. Several smaller diamonds glinted and reflected off the shining gold band encasing the marquis shaped stone.

"It fits you, Nikki. You fit me. I want to come back to you as my wife, after I complete my Officer training."

"Yes, Will. Oh, yes! I love you so much!"

She pulled him close to her and kissed him hard.

Chapter Twenty-Three

Valentine's Day. The day of love. David thought there was no more beautiful a vision, than his daughter. She stood before him in the dress her mother had worn twenty-five years earlier. It took all his strength to hold back the emotion he felt building inside him. Nikki looked so much like her mother did back then. She softly kissed his cheek before turning to take one last look in the full-length mirror of the dressing room.

She dreamed of wearing her mother's dress. It was simply exquisite. The halter style bodice consisted of virgin white satin, with pearls around the throat. It flowed into an empire waist, tight enough to enhance her figure. The bottom flowed out in layers of satin and tulle that trailed two feet behind her.

She wore a long cascading veil attached to a comb, held tightly in her upswept hair. Her makeup was perfect, just enough to highlight her softly glowing features. Her naturally peach colored lips glistened in the sunlight beaming through the windows, as she and her father made their way to the back of the church, awaiting the signal for their grand entrance.

Her bouquet consisted of peach tulips and Gerber daisies, symbolizing the flowers Will brought her once before. She held them tightly, as she went over everything in her head.

"Okay, mom's dress is something old. Roxie's earrings are something borrowed. The hankie I have in my dress is something blue. Oh no, Daddy. I don't have anything new," she whispered to him, just before the wedding march began to play.

David reached in his pocket and took out a brand new penny. "You didn't think your old man would let you down, did you?"

"Never, Daddy. I know I can always count on you." David kissed his daughter on the cheek. They walked slowly down the aisle in perfect unison.

When they reached the front of the church, before continuing to the altar, she stopped to kiss both mothers. Allison sobbed tears of joy when she looked up into her daughter's eyes. Mary Ann winked at Allison as they silently blessed the union of their beloved children.

Will felt his knees weaken when he saw her for the first time. Nikki's beauty made him defenseless. She radiated love as she walked down the aisle toward him. She stood quietly with her father while the organ continued to play. As her father gave her to Will, she slid her arm into his, squeezing tightly. He patted her hand gently with his, as they walked up the steps to the minister.

Missy and Roxie were already emotional. They stood together next to her, stifling their tears. Will tried to maintain control when he repeated his vows to Nikki. He hesitated as a tear rolled down his cheek. Nikki squeezed his arm to comfort him as he finished speaking. Her voice shook when her turn arrived. They held hands tightly as the ceremony was completed.

"Draw sabers," announced the honor guard officer.

Silently, each saber of the eight uniformed honor guard members cut the air forming the 'Arch of Sabers'.

The newly married couple entered the arch before their first kiss, as husband and wife. When the kiss finally ended, both Will and Nikki saluted the honor guard at the end of the arch. Turning to exit the arch, Nikki slid her arm through Will's, as the members of the honor guard sheathed their sabers. Boothe quietly swatted Nikki's bottom with his saber on her exit, completing the final Marine Corps tradition.

Surprised, Nikki turned to frown at Boothe, as the congregation roared with laughter.

"I forgot about that," she said laughingly.

"Boothe has been waiting to do that his whole life," Will told her.

"I'm so glad that I could make his day."

Will swept her up into his arms.

"I love you, Spunky."

"I love you most."

Epilogue

"You know, Lieutenant, I'll be glad when you get home so you can appreciate the green tinge that has now taken over my face. I would've never let you impregnate me if I knew I was going to toss my cookies every five minutes," Nikki said when Will answered the phone in his barracks at Quantico.

Two days earlier, Will became a 2nd Lieutenant in the United States Marine Corps. Two months prior to that, Nikki found out she was pregnant. Will was thrilled that Nikki was with child. He couldn't wait to get back to England, and experience the remainder of her pregnancy along with her.

Will worried about her being home alone. However, since Roxie and Aaron arrived, Nikki's needs were well taken care of. Roxie and Aaron now occupied Nikki's house since Nikki had moved in with Will.

Nikki loved having family close by as her body began going through a monumental changes. Nothing was the same. Her skin was different. Her hair was different. Roxie became a sounding board whenever Nikki felt unpleasantness.

"I'll be home before you know it, Darlin'. I have really missed you. I could care less if you were purple. I'd still want to jump your bones," Will replied.

"I don't think I can stand any of your extracurricular activities for a while. It wouldn't be too sexy if I had to run to the toilet during our climax."

"Well, maybe you're right. That might turn me off a bit—on second thought—"

"Do you know that you're a pig?"

"Yeah, but you married me."

"So I did. Just hurry home, okay? I really miss you. Junior here wants to hear his daddy's voice."

Clearing his throat, Will swallowed the lump that formed there. "Damn, that sounds wonderful. Daddy."

"Don't you start getting teary eyed on me William Chambers. I'm emotional enough as it is. I know once you've started the water works, that will be the end of me."

"Okay. I'll save the teary reunion for when you meet me at the train station. I'll be in at 4:09 Sunday."

"I'll be there with bells on. Or should I say, booties?"

ONE OF THE FEW

Prologue

Roxie held Aaron as he threw his last handful of birdseed over the heads of his newly married cousins. They waved their good-byes and Roxie headed back into the church leaving Aaron with her mother. She spotted him. He was standing up against the wide column in the atrium with his ankles crossed and his hands in the pockets of his uniform pants. Smugly, he removed his white gloves and placed them inside the shiny white cap then held it under his arm, while never taking his dark eyes off of her. Turning quickly, Roxie's knees buckled when the point of her stiletto heels caught in the grout of the tiled floor. Regaining her composure, she continued walking on to avoid another confrontation with Boothe O'Brien.

"Ya leavin' me without tellin' me good-bye?" Boothe said in that slow Georgia accent thick as molasses.

"I needed to get Nikki's and my things, and the unity candle from the altar," Roxie said, attempting to control the tremble in her voice.

Before Roxie could react, Boothe grabbed the back of her neck and pulled her into him. His mouth enveloped hers, parting her lips with his insistent tongue. Roxie moaned slightly as she gently pulled away. Her lashes fluttered and she looked up at him in a daze. *I knew he'd be a great kisser*, she thought to herself.

Roxie attempted to shun his advances last night at the rehearsal dinner when she kept finding his hands touching hers in a most infuriating manner. It seemed that whenever her hands reached for something at the table, there he was grabbing for the same thing with his big, powerful fingers covering hers. She pulled away from him quickly several times leaving him smirking at her in that dangerous way he had about him.

Thankfully, Roxie did not have to walk down the aisle with him during the ceremony. However, she had been paired up with him after the "arch of swords". As the best man he was given the duty of slapping Nikki across the backside as she and Will exited the arch. Boothe was beside himself with excitement after fulfilling his responsibility. Furious, Roxie walked back down the aisle with him using all the control she could muster not to kick him in his arrogant balls!

During the entire ceremony, she could feel the heat from those gorgeous eyes of his searing through her skin. It was nerve-racking! Roxanne McNamara would be glad to get back home to Texas and away from that man as quickly as possible. Hopefully, by the time she returned in the fall, he would be stationed somewhere else. She could tell that Boothe O'Brien was nothing but trouble.

Chapter One

"Oh, yeah," Boothe said as he thrust again into the wet pussy of Mandy, his date for the evening.

"Fuck me, Boothe. You are such a good fuck!" She squealed as the tops of his thighs slapped against her buttocks.

Boothe's hard dick pounded its way deeper into her dripping pussy. Fucking had always been, and would always be, his favorite pastime. The wetter the cunt, the better he liked it. Fortunately for him, every woman on Menwith Hill patiently waited to be his "lady of the evening". Boothe held a reputation for making a woman feel like a woman better than anyone else on the base.

"God, Boothe. Your dick feels so incredible," Mandy replied as she pressed her ass into him in circular motions.

Boothe reached around, cupped her breasts and pulled her nipples, causing a slight twinge of pain, as he continued ramming her from behind.

"Hang on, babe," Boothe said as he pulled out of her pussy and pushed his heated erection into her ass, completely.

"Yes, yes," Mandy screamed as she pressed into him. "Yes, Boothe, fuck my ass!"

Mandy's ass tightened around his cock like a glove. He pulsated in her as she continued to scream in ecstasy. He pulled out his cock and re-entered, slamming into her with full force.

"God, Boothe. Oh...my..." Mandy said before collapsing on the bed.

It wasn't the first time Boothe had made a girl pass out. In fact, this was number fourteen, if his memory served him correctly. If you were one of the lucky ones whose fucking enjoyment led to a loss of consciousness, you held a special place in Boothe's little black book.

He removed the condom from his heaving prick and rolled off the bed. Mandy lay in a heap on the bed. Boothe snickered to himself as he gently turned her over and kissed her taut nipples in an attempt to rouse her.

Mandy blinked her eyes open and stared at him in amazement.

"Did I pass out?" she asked him in disbelief.

"Yea, you did."

"Oh, God, Boothe. I'm sorry," Mandy said trying to hide her embarrassment. "I had heard you could do that, but I never thought I would be one that would actually do it."

"Hey, babe. It just proves you were really into the moment."

"I'll say," she said softly before being interrupted by the ringing telephone.

"Yea," Boothe said as he picked up the receiver.

"Boothe, you weren't screwing somebody, were you?" Nikki asked him from the other end.

"Um, not exactly," Boothe said smiling.

"Never mind. I don't even want to know," Nikki said to him. "I have a big favor. Roxie is coming in this afternoon, and I really need you to pick her up for me. Phil and I have a meeting with some guys from Saudi and her train comes in at 3:30. Can you help me out?"

"Sure, Nik. I'll be there. I'm sure Roxie isn't going to like it too much, though."

"Just behave, if it's at all possible. Pick her up and bring her home. Don't try to cop a feel, and keep your dick in your pants, okay?"

"Nikki, I'm hurt. I can be a gentleman when I want to."

"Yea, Boothe, but unfortunately, I'm the only one that knows that."

* * * * *

After going through customs with a screaming toddler, nothing could stop her. Or that's what she thought.

Aaron loved the train ride. He looked out the window and oohed and aahed at everything. Roxie could finally relax. She was here. Thankfully, here was 6,000 miles away from John McNamara. No more looking over her shoulder. No more unexplained bruises that kept her in the house and away from her friends for days on end. She might even be able to regain her self-confidence and not be afraid of loving a man again. Best of all, her neighbors would be Nikki and Will Chambers.

Her cousin, Nikki, was more like a sister to her than anything. Will was Nikki's knight in shining armor and loved her more than anything else in the world. Nikki was expecting their first child and Will was attending Officer Candidate School in the states and wouldn't be home for six months. Roxie planned on helping Nikki through her pregnancy until Will returned.

Unexpectedly, a flash of Boothe O'Brien flickered through her memory. She rubbed her fingers across her lips remembering the feel of his kiss. Roxie thought of him many times since the wedding. She tried not to, but the damn man even entered her dreams, on many a night. Boothe scared the shit out of her! He was a dangerous looking man with jet black hair, dark brown eyes, and olive skin. He was six feet of muscular manliness, with chiseled features that made her pulse quicken every time he looked at her. But in her eyes, he might as well be Satan. She definitely avoided him like he was the antichrist when they were in the wedding, and that was going to continue.

Boothe O'Brien never had problems getting women. They were drawn to him like bees to honey. Now this particular Texan bee acted like he had no honey, and showed no sign of changing. His usual flavor had big tits, no brains, and would open her legs to the slightest innuendo. Boothe O'Brien didn't hunt for women, they came to him, in more ways than one. He had a reputation for being the best fuck any woman could imagine, and he liked it.

Since before the wedding and much to his surprise, visions of Roxie popped into his head at the damnedest times. Like when he was about to kiss someone else, he remembered what she tasted like. Roxie McNamara drove him crazy and she didn't even know it. His sex life was going down the tube and he bet little Miss Roxie slept, ate, and went on with her life just fine. Shit, she wasn't even in the country and yet there she was. *How many cold showers could a man take until it did permanent damage to his libido?* he wondered, as he pulled into the train station.

Boothe waited to the side of the platform knowing if she spotted him first, she might bolt. Hearing a commotion similar to someone being arrested, he looked up to see Roxie coming off the train, followed by her entourage of faithful male followers.

She doesn't even know she's beautiful, Boothe thought to himself. What was it about this one woman that made men lose their fucking minds! Boothe's chest tightened uncontrollably at just the sight of her coming off the train.

The conductor carried two rather large suitcases. One passenger, obviously smitten with Roxie's presence, trailed her like a terrier in heat. Boothe snickered when he envisioned the prick humping her leg uncontrollably.

Roxie paused on the platform with Aaron in tow, clinging to his small suitcase and a filthy shred of silky material. Ignoring the men's futile attempt to vie for her favors, an exhausted Roxie looked around desperately for Nikki, when she spotted Boothe.

Sashaying over to her, Boothe leaned down and kissed her on the cheek.

"Hey, gorgeous. You need some help?" Boothe said giving her roadies his best "I'm a Marine" look, making them slowly back off.

"Thanks for taking care of the little lady, but I'll take over from here."

His smile seemed more like a snarl to the men who now pretended nothing happened, and continued on their way.

"Hey, kid. Want to ride on my shoulders?"

Aaron squealed as Boothe picked him up over his head.

"Look, Mommy. I'm bigger than you!"

"I don't know what happened in there. One minute it was me and Aaron and the next, three men were picking up my bags and helping me off the train," Roxie said, still a bit unnerved.

"Where's Nikki?"

"She got held up at work so I agreed to come and get y'all. I hope you're not too disappointed."

How could anyone be disappointed with a man whose ass looked like that in jeans, thought Roxie with a sigh as she followed Boothe. He actually caused her mouth to water. Resisting him would prove to be more difficult than she envisioned.

Chapter Two

Roxie slid out of bed and headed downstairs as quietly as she could so as not to wake up Aaron. She loved her son dearly, but she had to have some coffee before the fifty questions started. She looked around the house she absolutely loved and worked on a list of things to do.

Aaron would have so much fun playing in the yard. Roxie could let him run wild out there whenever he wanted because she could see him from any room in the house. The front yard had a fence with a gate she could close. She didn't want to be a hovering, overprotective mother. It would be a hard habit to break.

Mosquitoes and flies didn't seem to be a problem here, like in the States, so she could leave the doors and windows open, letting fresh air in as often as she wanted to. Maybe she would even buy Aaron a dog. He needed a companion to grow up with. Yes, their life would be better. She was sure of it.

Roxie was on her second cup of coffee and was making breakfast when she heard Aaron coming down the stairs. She rushed out to make sure he didn't fall and break his neck.

"Mommy, I'm up! Mommy, I'm up," he said.

Aaron was a happy child who seemed well adjusted, despite his prick of a father. Roxie scooped him up and kissed him all over his freckled face as he giggled hysterically. It was hard to believe you could love a little person so much. Even though her marriage ended in disaster, she was thankful she received Aaron out of the deal. Now, she couldn't imagine life without him.

* * * * *

Roxie stepped off the bus with Aaron on one hip. With her free hand she attempted to pull the umbrella stroller free from the pole next to the driver. She popped the stroller open, plopped Aaron in and buckled the restraints. Perspiring slightly, she wheeled him in front of Menwith Hill and through the gate, to the MOD police office. A nice looking, however, mischievous looking man, of about twenty-eight with shocking red hair was smiling at her.

"What can I help a pretty little thing like you with, love?" The man stared hard at her as she tried to avoid his shocking blue eyes to answer his questions.

"I'm new here and I need to register to get access to the base," Roxie told him, as his eyes continued to look her up and down.

"How about me showing you around? We could get a drink at the pub later," the officer said, as he handed her back her passport.

Last time I looked I didn't have "Fuck Me" stamped across my forehead.

"That's okay. We can manage. I'm meeting my cousin for lunch," she said

"Maybe tomorrow, then. I wouldn't want one of those bloody Marines to snatch you up first. They'd eat you up like candy."

He casually brushed his fingers down her forearm. "The name's Jeremy. You can ask for me whenever you come through," he said.

"No one is going to be eating me up," she said, annoyed as he continued to ogle her. "Look, all I need to know is what forms I have to fill out to be able to get on base. If you could just help me with this, I could get on with the other ten million items on my list," she said, grabbing the passport away from him. *Can you imagine what our children would look like? God help us. We would have Pippi Longstocking or Carrot Top!*

✽ ✽ ✽ ✽ ✽

The club on base served as a popular hangout for civilians, military, Americans, and the British as well. The homey pub-like atmosphere welcomed anyone that entered through its doors. Weekly "theme" nights offered an exciting change of pace for those who frequented.

Roxie was famished and didn't take any time to enjoy the view, but searched quickly for her cousin. Nikki waved excitedly when she spotted them. Aaron kicked his tiny legs frantically. Roxie unhooked the strap, he ran to Nikki, and jumped in her lap.

"Oh, be careful, honey," Roxie said as she got to the table. "You don't want to hurt Nikki."

"How are you feeling today?" Roxie asked her.

"It's hard to decide what to wear every day to match my green complexion," Nikki said, laughing and sipping the cup of herbal tea she ordered.

"That part should be over soon. I know it seems like forever. Aaron made me puke my guts up every day."

"What about being tired all the time? By the time I got home from your place last night, I could hardly hold my eyes open and it was only 7:30."

"I thought you looked a little frazzled," Roxie said, patting Nikki's hand. "Unfortunately, you might as well get used to it. Sleep as much as you can now, because when that baby gets here, you won't even remember what a good night's sleep is."

"Well, that's comforting to know," Nikki said disappointedly.

Chapter Three

"You are such a chicken! Just call him and get it over with," Roxie scolded herself. She knew Boothe would be at work. This would be an opportune time to call him. He'd be busy and wouldn't have time to chitchat with her. She could say her thank-yous and good-byes quickly and be done with it, so she thought. She noticed her fingers trembling slightly, as she dialed the numbers on the phone. It rang loudly in her ear, and she was just about to hang up, when someone answered. Roxie swallowed hard as she cleared her throat, and asked to speak to Boothe. Her stomach was doing flip-flops. *Good God!*

"Hey, Boothe," the voice on the other end of the line yelled. "One of your broads is on the phone. This one sounds pretty skittish so I'd be careful or you might scare her away."

"Lieutenant O'Brien," he said gruffly, jerking the phone out of the dispatcher's hand.

Her knees began to buckle so she sat down, hard, on the chair by the telephone.

"Boothe, this is Roxie," she said trying to sound calm and collected.

A shot of electricity went through his loins at the sound of her voice. A quick flash of her lying in his bed with all that beautiful auburn hair spread out across his pillow, jolted him, as he tried to regain his composure. With a hard thump, Boothe sat down.

"Hey, gorgeous."

"Um...I just called to say thank you for picking us up yesterday. We were exhausted and I don't know what we would have done if you hadn't taken care of us."

"It was my pleasure, Darlin'. Are you two settling in okay?"

"There is so much paperwork to become legit at that place. I plan on coming up there to finish it all up. Aaron already loves eating at the club, so I have to take him to lunch. It won't be long before he discovers there are fast food restaurants in Harrogate."

"Well, maybe I'll see you up on base sometime," Boothe said to her.

"Okay. Well, thanks again."

"Anytime, gorgeous."

Roxie nearly stepped on Aaron as she turned around. No one had ever called her that before. Gorgeous.

John insisted on calling her Roxanne. He was always so formal. God forbid he ever had any term of endearment for her.

"What would my little man like for breakfast this morning?"

"Fru oops," he said smiling up at his mother.

"Fruit Loops it is."

* * * * *

Boothe caught sight of Roxie as she pushed the stroller carrying Aaron in front of the club. His heart skipped a beat at her pure and natural beauty. He shook off the tingling in his loins as just a physical attraction, due to the fact he hadn't had a really good fuck in a couple of days. Women hadn't seemed to interest him lately. He had dated just about every unattached woman on the base. Recently, however, his love life suffered, somewhat, from a dry spell he conveniently blamed on working too hard.

Roxie walked into the club carrying Aaron on her hip. She scanned the room for an empty table. Finding none, she decided to have lunch at *Uncle Sam's*, the sandwich shop across the street.

Suddenly, Boothe felt like having a steak and cheese sub.

Roxie sat in a booth facing the door. Aaron sat in a booster seat on her right. She looked down as she cut up Aaron's pizza.

"Boo," Aaron yelled.

"Well, boo to you too," Roxie said not looking up.

"No, Mommy. Boo," he said again pointing at the door.

Roxie looked up and locked eyes with Boothe.

"Hello, gorgeous. Nice to see you," Boothe said as he bent down and kissed her on the cheek.

Roxie could feel her pulse and hear her heart beating in her ears. When he kissed her, it felt like lightning striking, sending electric shocks through her system. Her mouth dropped slightly as she envisioned herself melting in Boothe's arms, to do his bidding.

"Hi, Boothe," she said as her face reddened.

Boothe sensed that her pigment change was not from the stifling heat of the building but from his presence. He prided himself in making women sweat...in, and out of his bed.

"Mind if I join you?" Boothe asked, as he shook Aaron's tiny hand.

"Sure," Roxie replied sliding Aaron's plate in front of him.

"So, did you get all your paperwork finished?"

"Yes, finally. That was such a pain. You practically have to sign your life away to drive on this base! I didn't even have to register a car because I'm going to drive Will's jeep. It still seemed to take forever."

Roxie began to relax a little as she and Boothe discussed their days. Boothe made every attempt to include Aaron in the conversation. Aaron in turn only threw four French fries in Boothe's face. Boothe didn't seem to mind. Rather, he laughed and acted like the French fry monster and gobbled them up, making Aaron giggle incessantly. Roxie caught herself laughing out loud several times at the two of them. Boothe reached across the table and captured her hands in his.

"You have a beautiful laugh and smile, Roxie. You should do both more often," he told her as he smiled at her.

"Thank you. I think," she said as she looked down quickly and pulled her hands away from his.

"Why is it that every time the conversation turns to you, you tense up?"

"I just don't feel comfortable getting compliments."

"I've seen men look at you, Roxie."

She raised an eyebrow at him flirtatiously.

Boothe laughed and kissed her hand before she could stop him. The tingling of his lips on her skin shot up her arm and straight to her heart, making it beat faster, and unsteadily. *God, he was sexy. The way he looked at her made her stomach do flip-flops. Why couldn't she be like other women and just screw him? Then, she could get him out of her system and go their separate ways. Noooooo. Damn it! She had morals. There had to be feelings, and commitment, to get involved with someone. What would your son think about you when he realized his mother had no moral fiber?*

"You'd better hurry up, Roxie. Your son's head is about to fall in his pizza," Boothe said smiling, noticing the shock in her eyes, as she watched Aaron's head bob up and down, and then to the side of the table. She hadn't even noticed he had fallen asleep. Poor little guy.

"Exactly how long does it take until your body is used to this time zone? I'm so tired of falling asleep at five o'clock in the afternoon."

Boothe laughed at her comment. "Give yourself about a month. Each day make yourself stay up a little longer and do the same to him," he said pointing at the bundle she sat gently in the stroller.

Boothe felt a tiny pull in his stomach as he watched her backside wag in front of him as she buckled Aaron in.

"Roxie, how did you get on base?" he asked her as he looked out the window.

"The bus, why?"

"Shit, take a look for yourself," he said, pointing toward the window. "It's pouring outside and you two will get soaked, even if I take you to the bus stop. Why don't you drive my Land Rover."

"I really don't feel comfortable driving yet. I can call a cab if you'll take us to the gate."

"I still have some lunch time left. I'll just take y'all home," he said as he helped her on with her coat.

Roxie turned around to argue, but knew it would do no good.

Chapter Four

"Okay, buddy. Give it to me straight. Is Nikki really okay?" Will asked Boothe on the phone.

"Yea, dude. She's fine. I'd say the word was 'glowing'. Isn't that what *pregnoids* are supposed to be doing?"

"I guess. This is something I know nothing about. I just know that she'd never tell me anything bad over the phone. I really need you to keep an eye out for her, okay?" Will said.

"I told ya I would. Don't you trust me? I would never let anything happen to her, man. You know that." Boothe replied.

"Yea, I know. I guess I'm just a bit nervous, that's all."

"Trust me, Will. Nikki's the only chick who's safe with me." Boothe said. "By the way, you know Roxie is here, right?"

"Yea, and is that a problem for you?" Will questioned.

"No problem, if you don't mind going around with a fierce hard-on and blue balls that make you sweat. Not to mention the fact the woman looks at me like I'm her Uncle. I would even go for the scum of the earth, right now, it's at least something."

Will laughed at his friend's obvious infatuation with Roxie.

"Look, Boothe. Take it easy on her. She was married to the biggest asshole you can imagine, for way too long. She's probably just a bit gun shy, that's all." Will offered.

"I know I'd be a hell of a lot better off if I could just knock her down, sock it to her, and get a nut off. Maybe then she wouldn't bother me so much."

"Yea, you keep telling yourself that, dude. By the way, Nikki will eat you alive if you mess up her cousin. There will be nothin' left of you but a carcass when I get home, if you don't watch out."

"Yea, you're probably right. I've never met a woman who didn't want me. That's probably what's driving me crazy. If I could just fuck her, I could go on about my business," Boothe stated.

"Oh, Boothe, you're in looooove," Will teased him in a high-pitched voice.

"Fuck you! I got to go and check on your wife," Boothe said as he hung up the phone.

* * * * *

Nikki's head was buried in paperwork when Boothe walked into her office. The smell of onions and cheese caused her to salivate and jerk her head up from her desk.

"I brought you a surprise," Boothe said holding out the sub sandwich that she currently craved on a regular basis.

"Oh, Boothe, if I wasn't already knocked up by a Marine, I'd let you have your way with me," she said as she grabbed the wrapped sandwich from his hands, tore it open, and began devouring it.

"I haven't had time to spit, much less get lunch. Thank you," she mumbled with her mouth full.

"Will called and told me to make sure you weren't lying to him about how you were doing."

Nikki paused a moment, "Aw, isn't that sweet," she said batting her eyes at him, then delved back in to finish her sub.

"Are you sure that you're okay? You're not working too hard?"

"Yea, I'm great. After this week, I'm going to be working more from home and only coming in for meetings and stuff," Nikki said licking her fingers.

"Well, I'm just trying to be a good husband. You're probably the only wife I'll ever have."

* * * * *

Boothe's hands covered her breasts as she arched up to him. His thick shaft massaged her nub, now dripping with desire for him. His tongue teased her protruding nipples as she moaned and writhed with urgency for him to fill her. Suddenly, the moment was interrupted by his cell phone, ringing from his pants that lay on the floor, next to the bed. They tried to ignore the interruption, but the annoying ring continued over and over...

Roxie shook her head attempting to wake from the incredible dream. She glanced at the clock showing 5:30 a.m. She leaned over and answered the damn phone that brought her back to reality.

"Hello," Roxie said, listening to the clicks of the overseas operator coming across the line.

"Roxanne, you bitch! I can't believe you took my son to England. You just couldn't wait until I got back from my business trip, could you?" John McNamara said in a drunken slur. He had obviously spent his evening consuming large quantities of the scotch he adored. Considering it was 11:30 p.m. in Texas, Roxie could only assume he hadn't gotten lucky at the local bar. She would have to be the object of his abuse, as usual.

"Don't you mean vacationing with your boss, on company time," Roxie said as her stomach rolled. "Who do you think you're fooling? Everybody knows you sleep with her. You act like I snuck out in the middle of the night without letting you know. I told you months ago that we were leaving."

"I don't intend to pay child support for a kid I'm never gonna see," John said shouting at the top of his lungs.

"You don't pay child support on a regular basis, anyway. We don't need you, or your sorry ass money! That's what really gripes you, isn't it? You are pissed off because I haven't run back to you begging for forgiveness for leaving the great John McNamara. I don't have anything to say to you, especially when you're drunk off your ass," she said trying to swallow the bile rising in her throat.

"Roxanne, don't think I can't fly over there and knock the living hell out of you. I just don't have time right now. I will get more time off and when I do, I just might surprise you." He hung up laughing sadistically.

Roxie slammed the phone down and slumped down the side of the bed. She put her hands to her face and sobbed uncontrollably. The ringing phone startled her once again. She debated on answering it, afraid that it might be John again.

"Roxie, baby, is that you?" her mother's voice asked on the other end of the line.

"Mama, I'm glad you called," she said sniffing back her tears.

"You're crying. I'm too late, aren't I? That thug's already called, hasn't he?" Her mother asked, trying to console her.

"Yes, Mama. I just hung up with him. He was drunk, as usual, and everything was my fault. He even threatened to come over here and beat me up," Roxie said fighting back more tears.

"You know, I would pay good money to have that man disappear."

"I'm afraid you'll have to stand in line," Roxie said smiling now.

Alene Phillips hated John McNamara with all of her being. He had done more than enough to her baby. She could rip his heart out and watch him die, if it would do any good. She decided to get help for her baby girl and knew just who to call.

* * * * *

Nikki walked into her former abode to the smell of orange blossoms. She walked into the bathroom to find Roxie completely submersed in suds, with a washcloth covering her face.

"That bad, huh?" she asked her cousin.

"I take it you've talked to my mother?" Roxie asked removing the cloth from her face.

"My mother would call you if the tables were turned."

"You don't know any hit men on base do you? I could give them an assignment."

"I do, but ...if I tell ya I'd have to kill ya," both women said in unison, laughing.

"How about getting your wrinkled butt out of there and let's go to the club for dinner?" Nikki asked her.

"That sounds great, but my butt is not wrinkled!"

Chapter Five

As Nikki and Roxie were settling in at a table, Colin Meriwether, the base physician, stopped by on his way to being seated. Since he was dining alone, Nikki invited him to sit with them. She giggled to herself as he pressed himself firmly in the chair closest to Roxie, leaving two empty seats next to Nikki. It tickled her that Roxie was completely oblivious to this fact.

Boothe spotted Nikki's car in the club parking lot as he passed by heading for his barrack. He was in the mood for a beer, but this made it all the better if Roxie was with her. He rounded the corner and to his surprise the women and Aaron were not alone.

Uh oh, Nikki thought to herself.

Boothe's blood pressure rose slightly as he watched Roxie giggle and appear more attentive to Meriwether than Boothe felt necessary.

Nikki noticed the fire in Boothe's eyes and went in for the save. Smirking slightly, Nikki pushed her way between Roxie and Colin.

"Hey there, handsome. Where did you come from?" Nikki asked him smiling.

"Boo! Boo, Aaron up," Aaron said, holding his arms out to Boothe.

Boothe's expression changed instantly as the child pulled on his heartstrings. He bent down and picked the boy up from his booster seat.

"So, how's my temporary wife holding up?" he asked Nikki as he bent down and kissed her on the cheek. A slight twinge of jealousy flashed through Roxie when she realized he had bypassed kissing her completely.

"Other than being a bit green, I'm okay."

Boothe held out his hand to shake Meriwether's. "I haven't seen you in the club for some time, Meriwether," he said. Boothe fastened Aaron securely in his high chair and then placed his hand possessively on Roxie's shoulder. Boothe slid into the chair next to Roxie, leaving his arm draped across her shoulder.

"I just happened in and these beautiful ladies invited me to join them."

"What'cha eatin' there, kid?" Boothe asked Aaron.

"He's eating chicken tenders and green beans. However, the green beans seem to be dying of old age on his plate," Roxie said unhappy with her son.

"Yuk, Mommy. I no like beans."

"If you want chocolate cake, you have to eat your green beans, Aaron," Roxie stated, as firmly as possible.

Aaron picked up the light pink silk camisole that he had adopted as his security blanket. He covered his face with it thinking that if he can't see anybody, no one can see him either.

"Dude, what's up with this," Boothe said running the silk through his fingers. "Roxie, was this yours?" he asked her, feeling arousal rise up his chest at the thought of her wearing anything made of silk.

Blushing, Roxie sputtered out, "Yes, I wore it when I nursed him, he liked to rub the silk through his hands. If I wasn't wearing it, I had to drape it over my shoulder or else he wouldn't go to sleep. Now, he sleeps, eats and does everything else with it."

Just the thought of her breasts exposed made him hard as a rock. It disturbed him to no end the fact that she was speaking of nurturing her child made no difference whatsoever. He was ready to explode.

"I can deal with that. I think I'd be the same way."

"On that note, I should take my leave, ladies," Colin said bending down and taking Roxie's hand. "It was a pleasure meeting you, Roxie. I'll pick you up tomorrow around seven." Colin kissed Roxie and Nikki on the cheek before quickly departing the club dining room.

Did that British asshole just say that he was going to pick her up tomorrow?

Boothe could feel the heat rise in his chest at the thought of Roxie being with some other guy. *Shit, she wouldn't give me the time of day, but she'd go out with that limey?*

✱ ✱ ✱ ✱ ✱

"Will, listen to me. I'm not kidding. I think our Boothe has fallen head over heels for Roxie," Nikki told Will on the phone.

"Boothe O'Brien? The Boothe who you said you never wanted Roxie to get hooked up with? I can't believe it. I think being pregnant has made you delusional."

"I thought he was gonna kick Colin Meriwether's ass right there in the club," she said.

"Oh, I'm sure Roxie loved that."

"Yea, well, she's totally oblivious to the fact that Boothe wants to have wild monkey sex with her."

"Nicole Chambers, I can't believe you just said that. Are you trying to turn me on?" Will asked her trying to hide the fact that he missed her more than he ever thought he could miss another person.

"I would love to turn you on. However, I would rather wait until I can actually do something about it," Nikki said choking up.

"Oh, baby, please don't cry. You know I can't stand that."

"I'm sorry, Will. I just miss your ass so damn much!" she replied wiping her eyes.

"How are you and my baby? You know I miss you, too."

"We're fine. We just want you to come home. By the way, I have a sonogram next week. The doctor said that he would be able to tell the sex. Do you want to know?"

"What do you want to do?" Will asked her.

"I don't want to find out without you being there with me."

"I was hoping you'd say that. Let's be surprised together."

"Okay," Nikki said, as she closed her eyes contentedly listening to the sound of his voice.

"Take care of yourself, okay. Keep me posted on the Boothe and Roxie thing, too. I really think this is gonna be entertaining."

"Yea, me too," Nikki said giggling.

"I love you, Spunky," Will said. "I gotta go now."

"I love you most."

* * * * *

Boothe threw back his fourth beer in thirty minutes in an attempt to put the thought of Roxie completely out of his mind. If getting into a drunken stupor was the way to do it, then so be it.

"Hey, Boothe. Are you here alone?" Susan asked him seductively as she ran her fingernail up the back of his neck.

"Looks that way. You could change that if you'd like," he asked her as he pulled out a barstool for her to sit. What the fuck. Maybe getting his rocks off with *Spread-eagle Susan* might take his mind off the redheaded beauty.

Susan slid up the barstool in a way that gave Boothe a glimpse of her bare thighs, all the way up to her unclad cunt. Her bare nipples pressed through the lace of her blouse, beckoning Boothe to lay his hands on her.

"It's been a really long time, Boothe," she said, as she leaned into him.

Looking around the empty bar to make sure Gunny or any other Marines he knew weren't around, he put his knee between hers and slid his hand under her skirt.

"Yea, too long. How about we get the fuck out of here?"

Before they could get out of the door of the club, Boothe's rage over the situation blindsided him. He pulled Susan into the men's restroom locking the door behind them. As she gasped in surprise he turned quickly to put his back against the door and Susan in his arms.

"Easy, Boothe," she said as she unzipped his jeans. "We don't want to rush things now do we?"

"Yea, we do," he said as he guided her to her knees in front of him.

Susan giggled slightly, not too sure what happened to him, but willing to finish what they started, it was usually worth it. She released the full extent of his cock from his pants, enveloping it with her mouth. She could feel his desire thicken in her mouth as she continued to lave her tongue over the throbbing head. Boothe thrust into her throat as he held on to the sides of her head.

Susan moaned as she took him deeper into her mouth. She pulled him out at the exact moment that his juices released spewing all over her lips. She rubbed him up and down his thick shaft until his dick was empty.

She rose up rubbing herself on his dripping cock. She attempted to kiss his mouth, but Boothe pulled away.

"What's wrong," she whispered as she kissed his earlobe.

"I'm tired and I have a headache. I'm going home."

"That's it? What happened to the Boothe O'Brien who could make a girl pass out?"

"He's fucking pussy whipped," he yelled as he pulled his pants up and walked out the door leaving her behind.

* * * * *

"O'Brien, my office, now!" Gunny yelled through his office door the next morning.

Shit, what did I fuck up now? Boothe asked himself.

"Did you have a good time last night?" Gunny asked him motioning him to take a seat.

"Not particularly," Boothe replied wondering where this was heading.

"Well, neither did Susan Porter apparently. I got a phone call from her this morning accusing one Lt. O'Brien of conduct unbecoming to a Marine in the club men's room last night. Would you like to tell your side of the story?"

"Not really," Boothe said looking down at his boots.

"Let's put it this way, Lieutenant, I don't want to ever have one of your harem call me up again with all the gory details of your recent tryst. If you have a problem then either tell me about it or fix it. I know that Susan Porter has a bit of a…let's just say…reputation. I'm leaving it to you to handle. When your sex life interferes with your position as a Marine lieutenant, I will step in. Is that clear, Marine?"

"Crystal, sir." Boothe said, saluting before turning to leave.

Fucking hell, he muttered to himself. *I guess I've finally turned into the fucking pig that everyone says I am.*

* * * * *

The note attached to the bottle of wine he left on Susan's doorstep read:

Last night was a mistake.
Maybe you could share this with someone who will treat you right.
Boothe

Chapter Six

"Come in," Roxie said to Colin when she opened the front door.

"You look lovely, Roxie," he said as he kissed her lightly on the cheek.

Before anymore could be said between the two of them, Aaron ran toward them with peanut butter covering both hands, raised and ready.

Colin held his hands up to keep the child at bay as he dodged the mess covering Aaron's tiny fingers.

"What on earth?" she asked Aaron as she led him into the kitchen to clean up.

"Lovely child," he said unconvincingly. "Will he be joining us this evening?" Colin asked her with annoyance.

"No, Nikki's going to keep him." Roxie replied, a bit irritated that Colin was not as enamored by her son as she was.

* * * * *

During the ride to the pub, Roxie saw for herself why the 36-year old Colin Meriwether had never been married. He was boring as shit. If you put a lump of coal up his ass you would have a diamond. To top it all off, the kiss they shared before entering the pub made Roxie feel like she was kissing an uncle...her uncle, Mr. Limpett, the fish. There was absolutely no chemistry...at least not on her part.

Boothe O'Brien could just look at her with his dark eyes and make her lips tingle and goosebumps rise on her skin. The only thing Colin did to her skin was kind of make it crawl. Not to mention the fact he obviously did not care for children by the way he seemed completely put off by her son's actions. God forbid Aaron get peanut butter on his designer suit!

Colin pulled out her chair and they sat waiting to order drinks when his beeper went off.

"Dr. Meriwether," he replied, when he called into the hospital. "Damn, yes, I'll be there right away," he said looking irritated. "I'm sorry, Roxie. I hope you will grant me a rain check. I have an emergency at the hospital."

There is a God, Roxie thought to herself. "Oh, Colin, that's okay. Thanks anyway."

"I'll take you home before I go to the hospital."

"Oh, don't bother. I wouldn't want someone to die because of me. I'll call Nikki and she can come get me. You go and tend to your patient. We'll do this again..." *God, I hope not,* "...real soon. "

"You're a love, Roxie. See you soon," he said as he hurried out of the pub.

✳ ✳ ✳ ✳ ✳

"What are you doing here, Boothe?" Nikki asked as she opened the front door.

"I'm just checking on my wife. That's my job remember?"

"Boooooooooooo!" screamed Aaron as he peeked around the corner.

"Hey, kid. What are you up to?" Boothe said as he picked the boy up into his arms. Boothe nonchalantly looked down the hallway.

"She's not here, Boothe," Nikki said smiling.

"Who?"

"Yea, like you don't know who. It's me, remember? I know that you want to get in my cousin's pants."

"Why you want to wear Mommy's clothes, Boo?" Aaron asked angelically.

"Never mind, munchkin," Boothe said actually feeling himself blush.

Boothe was saved by Nikki's ringing telephone.

"Yea, Roxie, I'll be right there."

"What's wrong?" Boothe asked her.

"Colin had an emergency at the hospital. She needs me to pick her up."

"I'll handle it," he said handing Aaron over to her. "Are you okay with the munchkin? It looks like I'm going to get my date with your cousin after all."

"Boothe, you be nice," Nikki told him, looking a little worried.

"Always, Nik."

Chapter Seven

Roxie sat at a small table in the middle of the pub, sipping on a white wine. She checked her watch and looked toward the door just as Boothe stepped in.

Holy shit, she thought to herself, as she swallowed the huge lump that had lodged in her throat.

"Boothe, what are you doing here?"

"I'm saving you, that's what," Boothe said smiling. "Is the Doc too important to take a girl home? He just left you stranded here?"

"No, Boothe. I told him to go on and I would call Nikki. Where is she anyway?"

"She's at home with the munchkin. Have you eaten dinner yet?"

"Uh, no, but…"

"Good, I'm starving. Looks like me and you are finally going to have a date," Boothe said sitting down at the table next to her.

Roxie sat with her mouth agape staring at him in disbelief. "You don't have to do this, Boothe. I'll just make a sandwich at home."

"Are you ashamed of me, Roxie?"

"Why no, Boothe. Why would…"

"Are you embarrassed to be seen with me?"

"No, no, why —" Roxie said as she started getting more flustered.

"Because you always look at me like I've got two heads on my shoulders."

Surprised, Roxie gulped and tried to respond. "Boothe, I never meant to…that's hardly what I…I didn't intend…"

"See, you don't even know how you feel about me. Let me tell you something though. You are the prettiest thing I have ever seen, and I would really like to get to know you better."

"I'm surprised. I never knew you felt that way."

"That's what makes you so incredible. You don't even know how great you are. You are completely oblivious to the gawks and stares you receive everywhere you go. But I'm not. I've seen the way guys look at you. Check out that dude for instance." Boothe motioned to the man sitting behind Roxie and to her left. His tongue practically hung out of his mouth as he watched her sip her wine.

Roxie glanced behind her catching the man staring right at her. He blushed and turned away, quickly trying to pretend he wasn't ogling her.

"I guess I never thought of myself that way. I'm a mom and a divorced woman. That's it."

"Oh, no. That's far from it. I'd just like to show you how very different you are. Let's order dinner."

"So, Roxie, tell me everything about you," Boothe said sipping his coffee.

"Oh, Boothe, I'm just a plain person with nothing to tell you. Being here is the most exciting thing to happen to me in a really long time. You're the one with the hair raising life and career."

"You know my job's secret. But I can tell you that I am very close to my mama and sister, who are back in Georgia. I miss them very much. I've never been married or anything close to it. I like women…a lot. I like the way women feel and smell. I especially like the way you feel, smell, and taste. Do I smell oranges tonight? I could just eat you up you smell so good," he said as he kissed her cheek.

Roxie's face reddened when he pulled away from her.

"Boothe, you embarrass me. I don't know what to say or do when you say things like that. No one has ever said things like that to me before."

"Christ, Roxie, you were married and have a son. I'm sure your husband told you things like that," Boothe said lifting her fingers to his mouth and brushing his lips across her knuckles.

"Not really. I was right out of high school, and way too young to get married. John was four years older and he was tired of waiting on me to have sex with him. I should've listened to my parents. However, I thought I knew him better than they did. I was wrong," Roxie said looking away, as a tear escaped down her cheek.

Boothe took her chin in his hands and turned her face to him. He wiped the lone tear away with his thumb. "I had no idea. He must be a very stupid man to let you get away and not cherish every ounce of you. His loss is my gain. I plan to make up for his stupidity and romance you, if you'll let me." He kissed her gently on the lips.

"I'm sorry. I hate to cry over him. Nikki's the only one I ever talk about John to, and that's only on rare occasions. I don't want you to feel sorry for me. I hate people who wallow in self-pity and drag everyone down with them. I made a mistake. But, I have a beautiful son out of it, and that's all that matters to me. Let's talk about something else, okay?"

Roxie felt like a schoolgirl as they sat in front of Nikki's house inside Boothe's Land Rover.

"Thanks for coming and getting me," Roxie said trying not to look at his gorgeous dark eyes.

"I had a great time. How about if we have another date? You know, a real one where I pick you up and bring you home...or to my place. Whatever moves you."

"I think I'd like that, Boothe. I'll check with Nikki and see if she's up to keeping Aaron again."

"That sounds like a plan, gorgeous," Boothe leaned across the seat to her. He took her fragile chin in his hands and looked deep into her eyes. "You are beautiful. I want you to know that."

Boothe's mouth covered hers with a heat Roxie had never felt in her life. She could feel her breasts tingle at the play his tongue made with hers. Heat rose in her cheeks, and there was a telltale dampness starting between her legs. She could easily let herself go and give herself completely to him. That wasn't her, though. She wanted it to be right. She wanted someone to love her.

Chapter Eight

"I always wanted to have an attic room when I was a kid," Roxie said admiring the paint and wallpaper they just completed.

"Yea, we did a good job didn't we?" Nikki replied beaming as she looked around the room that would soon be filled with diapers, booties, and toys.

"So, do you think Boothe likes me?" Roxie blurted out.

"God, Rox. Are you kidding me? All you have to do is walk in the room and you can tell the boy is smitten."

"Really? I guess I just don't see it."

"Trust me, Rox. Everybody else does. I have known Boothe O'Brien long enough, and seen how he is with women, to tell you that all you have to do is snap your fingers and he would belong to you. Knowing him like I do, I can tell you, that says a great deal. No woman has ever had control over Boothe O'Brien," Nikki said wringing her hands.

"I love you both, Roxie. If I thought for a minute that Boothe would hurt you I would tell you to run the other way. Fact is, I didn't want him to get anywhere near you when I first met him. You would make him a better man, Roxie," Nikki said wiping away the tears that now formed in her eyes.

"Well, fuck! I hate to cry and since I've been pregnant that's all I seem to do."

"It's nice to have someone care about you so much," Roxie said as she hugged her cousin. "I may need you more, as things with Boothe and I heat up."

"Oh, don't worry. I want to hear everything. I've always wanted to know what he looked like underneath his skivvies, but I couldn't exactly ask Will, you know?"

"Well, if the size of the bulge in his pants the other night was any indication, the man is hung like a bear."

* * * * *

Boothe and Roxie entered the bar, just as a local band was setting up to play. After getting drinks, they found a small table in the back of the club.

"Come here," he said as he stood and held out his hand.

"Where are we going?" Roxie asked.

"I want to dance with you."

"Do you always get what you want?"

"Usually. Except you seem to be making it more difficult to have my way with you, than most women I've gone out with."

"Well, don't expect that to change anytime soon," Roxie replied, not too convincingly. The truth was, she wanted to have sex with him. However, the thought of sex without any kind of commitment was something she never considered with any man before. Roxie heard the rumors of Boothe O'Brien. Apparently, when a woman had sex with him, there was no substitute. She hated to admit it, but she was extremely curious about him.

Boothe held her into him as they danced. Her head rested comfortably on his chest, as their bodies swayed in unison. The smell of oranges wafted up to him, making his pulse race slightly.

No matter how much she hated to admit it, being wrapped in his arms was heavenly. Hearing his heartbeat quicken, she snuggled into him closer.

"Hey, Boothe. The song's over," someone yelled to Boothe.

They then realized everyone had left the dance floor but them. It amazed her that one man could make her completely oblivious to the world around her. She blushed with embarrassment as he led her off the dance floor. Staff Sergeant Michaels hunkered down slightly at Boothe's murderous gaze.

"Sorry big guy, but you were blocking my table. I've got my eyes on that chick over there, with the big...ahem, sorry ma'am," he said, looking down at his boots in embarrassment.

On the way back to their table, Roxie tried to control the bit of jealousy welling up inside her, as every woman in the club seemed to stop and greet Boothe. Most of them planting kisses on his cheek, or mouth, not even acknowledging her existence. Boothe enjoyed this attention too much for Roxie's liking.

Boothe noticed the irritability flash across Roxie's face. It humored him that she would let the attentions of other women bother her. That would mean she did like him more than she was letting on.

"Don't worry yourself, Roxie. We're all like family here."

"Yea, an incestuous family," she murmured under her breath.

"Let's get out of here," Boothe said, as he tossed enough cash on the table to cover the waitress' tip.

"Where are we going now?"

"To my place, of course. I'm tired of being interrupted and I can tell by the scowl on your face you are, too."

"I...I...don't think that's such a good idea, Boothe," Roxie said trying to pull her hand out of his.

"Chill out, Roxie. I'll take you home whenever you say and I won't do anything you don't want me to do. But, I think you want me to do more to you than you are letting on."

* * * * *

Boothe used his foot to kick the door to his barracks open. In one quick motion, he scooped Roxie up and threw her over his shoulder. He slammed the door shut with the sole of his boot before Roxie could respond.

"Boothe! What on earth are you doing?" Roxie yelled.

Before Roxie knew what happened he flopped her on top of the kitchen counter and stood between her legs.

"I'm sweating, Roxie. I'm going to change shirts if that's okay with you. I'll be right back."

Roxie sat on the counter perusing his tiny kitchen. Considering the fact he was a bachelor, she was surprised at how neat and tidy the countertops were. She smirked at the spoon rest that resembled a...yes, a pair of breasts. Only Boothe O'Brien would make such a purchase.

Boothe returned buttoning his shirt only halfway. Dark chest hairs sprang out making her breathing turn into a pant. Roxie actually thought she was going to pass out.

"Hello," Boothe said waving his hand in front of her face.

Roxie regained her composure quickly and spied the red scar rising from under the dark mat of hair.

"Oh, Boothe. How did you get that?" she asked him as she placed her fingers on the area just under his right nipple.

"Being in the wrong war at the wrong time."

Without thinking, Roxie bent down and kissed the injury. Boothe gasped for air in surprise.

"I'm sorry. I'm so used to kissing booboos to make them go away." Roxie blushed visibly. She couldn't believe she actually touched her lips to that rock hard chest of his. She could feel the tingle shoot through her body, making heat rise in her chest.

"Oh, darlin'. I'm not complaining in the least. That's just so out of character for you. One minute you're being Little Miss Innocent, and the next minute you're giving me a boner!"

It must have been a brief moment of insanity. Roxie pushed his shirt over his shoulders and slid her body down the front of him off the counter.

Boothe pressed her firmly up against the counter when he covered her mouth with his. Her lips parted to the beckoning of his tongue. She melted into him, feeling the stiffening of his cock press against the front of her. Her knees weakened and she almost lost her footing, before he grabbed her around the waist and pulled her even closer.

Boothe led her into his bedroom and lay her down gently on his unmade bed. The smell of him enveloped her, as she sank into his pillow. He rained kisses down the side of her neck and the front of her throat. His hands felt for the buttons of her blouse and with a skill Roxie found a little too perfected, he unbuttoned them all quickly leaving her heaving breasts exposed to his muscular chest.

His hands captured her breasts, peeling the material from her bra down to set her throbbing nipples free. Roxie threw her head back and arched into him. The sensuous moan that escaped her throat made his cock pulsate against the denim of his jeans.

Boothe flipped them over. She straddled the bulging mound between his legs and pushed herself into it harder. Her fingers ran over his chest and through the dark hairs that covered him.

"I love the way you feel," she told him as she continued to rub him. When her fingers reached his protruding nipples she pulled them slightly making him writhe with pleasure.

Boothe brought Roxie down, took her nipple in his mouth, and suckled her. Shivering, she moaned again as the pleasure of his tongue surged through her.

"You are incredible," he said to her as he turned them over.

They lay on their sides with her breasts pressing against his chest. Roxie flung her leg over his hips and pulled the bottom half of him into her.

"I have never wanted a woman as much as I want you, Roxie," he whispered in her ear. "It's scary."

"I want you to make love to me, Boothe. If you don't, I think I'm going to burst into flames," she said as she kissed his mouth fully.

"Shit fire and save the matches!" Boothe yelled when the phone rang.

"Let it ring, Boothe."

"Fuck! If I could, I would, but I'm on call."

Roxie lay on her back, enjoying the intense passion that consumed her while he was on the phone.

"Even though I could cut glass with my damn dick, Roxie, I have to go. I'm really sorry," he said throwing some clothes in his duffel bag.

"You're kidding, right?"

"I wish I was. I hope we can finish where we left off when I get back," he said as he ran his fingers along her jaw line. "I'm not sure when I'll get back, but I hope you'll be thinking about me."

"Unfortunately, I've done nothing but think about you every damn day I've known you. This just makes it more interesting. Please be careful and don't be a hero. I would love to finish this some day."

"Do you mind dropping me off at Ops, you can take my Rover home?"

"Okay, I'll bring it back tomorrow when I come back on base," she said longing to have his hands all over her once more.

As if reading her mind, he pulled her into him and kissed her thoroughly. Her knees buckled as she let his tongue ravage hers. Blinking away her blurred vision, she took his hand as he led her out of the door of his barracks.

* * * * *

Roxie always had vivid dreams. Tonight would be no exception. Boothe O'Brien made an appearance in every one.

Most of the time he was doing things to her that one only saw in porno movies. Not that she watched those nasty things. There had been one time that John insisted on it, hoping to loosen her up a bit. Little did he know that it only repulsed her.

Being the arrogant son of a bitch that he was, John never understood that if he showed her just the slightest amount of respect, she would have been his sex kitten. Boothe made her want to be that way. She wanted to let go of all her inhibitions.

The thought of Boothe made her entire body tingle with desire. Never had the thoughts of wild animal sex consumed her like they did now. All she could think about was feeling Boothe's strong arms around her, pulling her into him. The heat of his kiss seared through her like a torch in the night. Closing her eyes, Roxie remembered how Boothe made her feel before he left.

Roxie would have thrown caution into the wind if that damn phone hadn't rung. She would have given everything to him, even without a commitment from him.

She knew his history. Boothe surely only thought of her as a woman to be conquered. Roxie thought she knew what she was getting herself into. Something told her heart that this time Boothe would realize that she was different. What the hell, and it wouldn't rain tomorrow. She could use a good screw like any other normal young woman, couldn't she? Maybe this time, Boothe would be the one who would be used and abused.

✻ ✻ ✻ ✻ ✻

Boothe leaned his head back and closed his eyes as the chopper took off. He smiled from ear to ear.

"Boothe, I know Marines thrive on conflict, but I don't think I've ever seen a guy smile like that before a mission," Gunny said punching Boothe in the shoulder.

"Trust me, Gunny. This smile has nothing to do with a military mission," Boothe said closing his eyes again.

"What? That's all the info you're going to tell us? You always like to brag about your latest conquest."

"Sorry, this time it's my little secret," Boothe said.

"Uh oh, guys. I think Boothe's in love," Gunny said to the other crewmen.

Not arguing, Boothe continued to picture Roxie in his mind.

"Love...? Nah, not me. I'm just savoring the moment."

Chapter Nine

"Hi, gorgeous. You miss me?" Boothe asked Roxie when she answered the phone.

"Boothe, I didn't expect to hear from you so soon. Are you okay? When are you coming home?" Roxie rambled on in surprise.

"I just wanted to hear that sexy voice of yours. I'm waiting to get on another chopper. I don't know when I'll be home though. You and Aaron take care of yourselves. Think about me. I'll see you soon. Bye," Boothe said and then waited for her reply.

"Be careful," Roxie said before hanging up. Her heart pounded in her chest at the sound of his voice. God, what this man did to her.

✳ ✳ ✳ ✳ ✳

Boothe and the rest of the Marines in the regiment were regulars in the pub just outside the base, *The Queen Anne,* for both lunch and dinner.

After landing, the Marines decided to grab a few beers before hitting the hay. Finding their way to Lily's table, the sexy, flirtatious, and curvy Scottish barmaid, the four men seated themselves awaiting her arrival to take their lunch orders.

Lily's job was to make the patrons want to return to the pub that she and her brother owned. However, it wasn't such a chore to make herself readily available to the four Americans who darkened the doors most days at noon, or in the evenings to fill their bellies with food and spirits.

Two of them, she noticed, wore wedding bands, one had a face that would turn milk into cheese, but the other...oh, how he made her thighs heat up when he entered the room.

She quickly scurried to the table when she noticed the young men come in and sit down.

"The usual, mates?" Lily asked as she smiled at each of them seductively.

"Yeah, and why don't you give me a little smooch. We've just gotten back from a mission and I've been missing you," Winston, the beauty challenged idiot, replied to Lily's question. "She wants me," he said as he watched her sidle away from the table, swiveling her hips as she went.

"You wish, you little twerp," Gunny replied. "We all know that it's Boothe she wants to fuck. She has her tits in his face every time we come in this joint. In fact, I'm surprised you haven't already fucked her, Boothe."

"What the hell are you talking about?" Boothe asked unknowingly.

"Don't give me that. You know exactly what I'm talking about. She would be sittin' in your lap callin' you sunshine, if you would give her a chance," Gunny snapped back at him.

"Yea, I guess so," Boothe replied, not focusing on the conversation. The only thing he wanted to do was get back to his barracks and call her. How could she grab hold of his heart in such a short time? He knew the other Marines were right. This wasn't like him. Hell, he didn't even recognize himself anymore. Every minute of every day, she consumed him.

Usually the one to razz his buddies, Boothe spent the last few days being the butt of all their jokes. He couldn't even give anything back because he knew they were right. He was whooped. The fucking woman had trapped him. She had him lock, stock and barrel. He wondered if she even knew what she had done.

* * * * *

"Did I wake you, Nikki," came Boothe's deep voice on the other end of the phone.

"Hey, Boothe. Are you home?" Nikki asked him.

"Yea, I just got in a few minutes ago. I need you to do me a favor," Boothe said.

"Okay, and what can a pregnant woman do for you?"

"I want to surprise Roxie so I was wondering if I could get the key to her house from you," he asked her apprehensively.

"You, Boothe O'Brien, want to surprise a woman? What in the hell has gotten into you? I thought you were the one who received all the surprises from women," Nikki asked him teasingly.

"Yea, well, things change. Your cousin has made me crazy. I can't seem to stop thinking about her. I'm sure I don't need to tell you how surprised and pissed off that makes me."

"Oh, Boothe, you're going to make me cry. In fact, everyone seems to be making me cry lately."

"So, will you help me or what?"

"Yea, I'll help you. But, if you screw her over, Boothe, you're going to have to face my raging hormones and me. Got it?"

"Okay, Nikki. Don't get yourself in a tizzy. I'll be nice. I promise."

"Boothe, you are really scaring me now. You have never acted nice or even said the word before."

"Okay. If I told you that I have a dick a mile long and I want to fuck her brains out would that make you feel better?"

"Now that's the Boothe I know and love."

* * * * *

Boothe stood in the doorway to her bedroom watching her as she slept. Her disheveled mass of red hair splayed across her pillows. God, she was beautiful, even if she did have on a flannel nightgown that covered every inch of her.

Quietly, Boothe removed his clothes. The chill in the room made his nipples tighten. It was the sight of her and not the chill that hardened his cock. He shivered slightly as he slid under the covers next to her. He slowly pressed his body up against the warmth of her.

Suddenly, Roxie's eyes popped open to find him staring at her.

"Boothe," she whispered. "How did you get in here?"

"I had a little help from a friend," he said as he pulled her into him.

"Nikki," Roxie said laughing slightly.

"I've missed you, Rox. I didn't want to wait until tomorrow. You're not mad, are you?"

"No, I'm not mad. It's just…that…" Roxie stuttered.

"What is it?"

"I'm on the rag, Boothe," Roxie said blushing.

"Aw, fuck!" Boothe said, falling back on to the bed and rubbing his hands over his face.

"I'm sorry," Roxie replied, patting his cheek gently.

"You can't help it. I guess that thought never crossed my mind."

"Does that mean you have been thinking about me since you've been gone?" she said running her hands along his chest.

"Damn, girl, I haven't been able to think of anything but you. I hope you're happy." Boothe couldn't believe that a woman made him this mushy.

"You know you're going to owe me for this, right?" he asked her as he played with the ends of her hair.

"I figured you'd want to cash in at some point."

"Look, I can't believe I'm saying this. But, I just want to hold you the rest of the night. Would that be okay?" Boothe asked her, disgusted at how sappy he'd become.

"I think I could manage that," Roxie spooned into him, wrapping his hands around her waist.

This event had to go in Boothe O'Brien's record book. Never, never, ever, did he share a woman's bed if his dick was not satisfied. What in the hell was happening to him? He was actually going to spend the night, and not have sex with the woman who has been haunting him, for the last three days. Usually it was the opposite. He'd have sex and not spend the night. This reflected way more of a commitment than he'd been ready to make. When did his life make a complete three-sixty? The day that Roxie McNamara entered it, that's when.

Chapter Ten

"Boo, Boo, why you seepin' with Mommy?" Aaron asked Boothe, peeling back his eyelids.

A smile spread across his face as he rubbed the top of Aaron's head.

"I'm afraid of the dark, kid," Boothe whispered back.

"I am hungy, Boo," Aaron said looking up at him with his big brown eyes.

"Well, let's don't wake up Mommy and I'll get you something," Boothe said, swinging his legs over the bed, forgetting that he was wearing nothing underneath the sheet, and stood up.

Aaron stood, mouth agape, staring at Boothe's appendage. He only guessed what was going through the kid's mind.

"Don't even go there, kid," Boothe said grabbing up his haphazardly discarded pants from last night.

✳ ✳ ✳ ✳ ✳

The fragrant aroma of coffee brewing woke Roxie from her deep slumber. She felt across the bed to see if Boothe still joined her. Finding nothing, she wondered if it had all been a wonderful dream. Hearing her son's laughter downstairs, she decided to go see if it was, in fact, only her imagination.

The two of them sat across from each other at the dining table. Boothe sipped his coffee and read the newspaper. Aaron ate his cereal and pretended to read his Postman Pat book.

Roxie's heart flip-flopped in her chest as she watched them.

"Well, I see you two have everything under control in here," she said as she stood behind Aaron and placed her hands on his shoulder.

"Did Boothe get your breakfast for you?" she asked Aaron as she bent down to kiss him.

"Yea, Mommy. We mans. We can fix our own breffast."

"Hey, where's my morning kiss?" Boothe asked her coyly.

Roxie walked around the table and bent down to peck him on the cheek. Boothe had other plans. He grabbed her around the waist and pulled her down on his lap. He kissed her along her neckline, making her squeal with laughter. Aaron thought the sight of his Mommy giggling to be hilarious, and yelled with laughter along with her.

"Hey munchkin, I brought you and Mommy a present while I was gone. You want to go with me to the car and get them?"

"Yey, prezzies! I go," Aaron said squealing down the hallway.

Tears formed in Roxie's eyes at the thought of Boothe O'Brien, the base stud, buying presents for a toddler. The man didn't cease to amaze her.

"Look, Mommy, look," Aaron screamed holding a toy Hum-V in the air above his head.

"Here's yours, gorgeous," Boothe said holding out a box of rich, gooey chocolates.

"Boothe, these are expensive. But, I'll eat them just the same." Roxie popped one in her mouth and her eyes rolled back in her head.

"Well, gorgeous, I've got to get to work. See ya later, kid." Boothe said as he rubbed the top of Aaron's head.

Roxie walked him to the door.

"So, exactly how many days is it going to be before I can get in your pants?" Boothe asked her, before kissing her thoroughly.

"That's classified information," Roxie said, smiling as she closed the door.

* * * * *

"This is for my godchild to remember his, or her, roots," Boothe said to Nikki as he kissed her on the cheek. He handed her the bear, dressed in Marine Corps fatigues, that he bought for her while he was away.

"This will be its first present," Nikki sobbed and wiped the tears from her cheeks. "Shit, I hate to cry. Why am I always crying?"

* * * * *

"Okay, spill it," Nikki said as she barreled through the door.

"I have three words for you. On...the...rag," Roxie said smirking at her cousin.

Nikki fell to her knees in uncontrollable laughter. "Rox, you're kidding. That is hilarious. If I'd known, I wouldn't have given him my key. Oh, God, I bet Boothe O'Brien has a serious case of blue balls!"

Chapter Eleven

Boothe sat at the poker table, cigar hanging out of the side of his mouth and dealer visor covering his eyes.

"Gunny, are you in or out?" Boothe asked as he dealt the cards.

"I'm in, you cock sucker. Pass me one of those beers."

Boothe continued dealing to Winston, Michaels, and a Marine they affectionately called Booger Red.

"Okay, you pussies, whose money am I going to take this round?" Boothe boasted as the game began.

Boothe's Wednesday night poker party was the Marines' time to relax, bullshit, and drink an abundance of alcohol. Considering all the men lived on the base, no one had to worry about drinking and driving.

"Shit," Boothe said when the phone rang. "Why does the goddamn phone have to ring during my goddamn poker game?"

"Yea!" he yelled in the phone.

"I'm ready for you," Roxie whispered through the phone line.

The cigar Boothe held in his teeth dropped in his lap as his dick hardened to the sound of her voice. Simultaneously, he opened the cards in his hand to a Royal Fucking Flush. Feeling the heat from his cigar burning through the material of his pants, he jumped from the table making it flip, sending cards, chips, money, and beer flying across the floor.

"What the fuck?" the men yelled in unison.

"I'm on my way," Boothe whispered to Roxie.

"You pussies can play, drink, fuck each other in the ass, I don't care. I'm outta here," Boothe said grabbing his keys and jacket and slamming the door to his barracks behind him.

"Marines," Gunny said getting the men's attention. "I think our Boothe's in love."

* * * * *

Roxie smoothed the pantsuit over her curves as she stood in front of the mirror. She couldn't actually believe she bought something as revealing as this. However, she knew the plunging neckline would only aide in her endeavors to get Boothe O'Brien in her bed. To screw this time.

"Shit!" Roxie exclaimed hearing the sound of Boothe's Harley pulling into her driveway. "He must've driven 95 miles an hour."

Roxie went to the window and looked down as he slowly dismounted from the intimidating heap of metal.

"Oh, my God!" Roxie said out loud, as she watched him.

Removing his helmet, Boothe slid his right leg across the seat. He smoothed his hands over the soft brown leather of the bomber jacket he wore. He had opted for his Harley this time, because he thought the cold air hitting his face would sober him up a bit before he got to her house. The Harley went a hell of a lot faster than the damned Rover anyway. Besides, they weren't going anywhere...except to heaven in her bed.

Roxie's blood ran hot as she watched him sidle his way up to the front door. Even though she anticipated the sound, she startled when the doorbell chimed loudly below her.

Roxie admired the man standing in her doorway. He wore a black t-shirt and red USMC sweat pants. She loved the way his clothes fit him to perfection accentuating every muscle and ripple that ran over his body.

Boothe's eyes followed the trail from her feet, all the way up her body, until they met her deep green eyes. Slowly, a smile formed on his lips, deepening the dimple on the right side of his face.

"Christ, Roxie. You're beautiful," he said to her as he slowly walked closer, closing the door behind him. The pantsuit left nothing to the imagination. He could see every luscious curve of her slender body.

"Where's Aaron?" he asked looking up the stairs.

"He's with Nikki. All night," she added as she looked at him sensuously.

"Do you have any idea what you are doing to me?" Boothe asked her.

"I would have to be blind not to notice," Roxie said as her eyes pointed to the tent that formed at the front of his sweatpants.

Roxie had never made a man blush before. She quite liked the feeling that it gave her. Power. Yes, she had a hold on the man. This was going to be fun. For once in her life, she had control of the situation. It flattered her that a man like Boothe, one so completely wrapped up in himself, could be brought down by a simple phone call from her.

Boothe was putty in her hands. She knew he would never admit it, but she could tell by the way he flew to her, she had him right where she wanted him. This time she made the rules.

He brought his mouth down to hers and kissed her deeply. She put her arms around his waist bringing them closer to each other. Boothe could smell the botanical lotions she obviously bathed in, and tasted the fresh mint of her mouth. He took the kiss deeper by wrapping his arms across her back and holding her there tightly.

His cock ached with desire as it pressed firmly into her. Never in his life had a woman made him ache. Women were toys to him. Not this woman, however. She made him pant like a dog, just by a whisper over the fucking phone line. God, he was pathetic. But, damn, this woman made him feel incredible.

Roxie reciprocated his moves, breath for breath, stroke for stroke, as they feasted on each other completely. Suddenly, she pulled away. Boothe moaned from deep in his chest.

"Damn, Roxie. I want the hell out of you," Boothe said as he scooped her up and carried her up the stairs. He nibbled and kissed her neck, making her giggle, incessantly.

"I hope you know that you are killing me. I don't feel panty lines on this beautiful ass of yours," he said, as he rubbed his hand across her firm buttocks.

"Thank heavens for thongs," she said raising her brow at him.

"Oh, God. You are going to kill me."

"Not intentionally," she said as she smiled up at him.

Boothe set her back down at the entrance to her bedroom.

"Are you sure this is what you want?" This was the first time Boothe ever asked a woman what she wanted. In his past encounters, Boothe took the invitation into a woman's home as being an invitation into her pants as well. No questions asked. However, Roxie's feelings mattered to him. More than he thought anyone's could. He wanted to love her but only if she was truly ready.

"I'm going to be very straightforward with you, Boothe," she said as she made herself keep looking into his dark brown eyes. "I've tried to fight the feelings I have for you, but I don't want to anymore. I don't want to be a one-night stand, a booty call or just one more of your base whores. Other than that, I'm not really sure what I want. I know that I want you, but I have to consider my son. He likes you too. I don't want to hurt him. Maybe after we get the sexual frustration out of our system, we will find out that we weren't that great for each other, and we can move on."

"Shit!" Boothe said laughing derisively.

"But I feel the same way as you, Roxie. I don't want a one-night stand either. I never thought I would hear those words come out of my mouth, but it's true. I would never disrespect you and make you feel like a whore. Lord knows I have tried not to think of you, but it just doesn't work. Hell, I even dream of you and that great body of yours. So, what do we do now?"

"Kiss me, you fool," she said as she moved into him.

Boothe moaned deeply. The kiss was soft, but soon his tongue parted her lips, in invitation to her depths. Their tongues rolled ravenously over the other. They continued tasting each other with all the heated passion that consumed them. Gasping for air, Roxie pushed away from him, looking at him with her sex-glazed eyes, she smiled at him.

"I'm sorry, but I couldn't breathe."

"I know what you mean," he said as he closed his eyes tightly for a moment. "Roxie, I want to make love to you."

Roxie stood, trying to control the shaking of her knees. She hoped Boothe wouldn't be able to hear them knocking together. She offered him her hand. Boothe took the slender fingers, bending them slightly to kiss her knuckles gently and lovingly. He put his arms around her waist and kissed her softly across her lips and down her slender neck. She envisioned butterflies softly batting their wings down her skin, as she closed her eyes and leaned her head back, to enjoy the moment.

The bedroom was aglow with what looked like a million candles. He wanted her more than he remembered wanting any other woman. In fact, he couldn't even remember any other woman. God knows there were many of them from his past. But, they were faceless now. Roxie was the only face he saw in his mind.

His senses were on fire, as much as the flames that twinkled from each candlestick. He laid her very gently on the bed and hovered over her, admiring her beauty. Boothe removed the clip from her hair and let his hands run through the auburn mass of curls. Roxie put her hands on his face, pulled his mouth down on hers, and hungrily kissed him. Their tongues did an erotic dance as they dove deeper into each other. Boothe swore he could feel her tongue tickling his tonsils.

"Darlin', slow down. I want to make love to you slowly. I want you to remember this night for a very long time."

Roxie looked at him and placed his hand on her breast.

"Boothe, I feel like I am on fire. I want you all over me."

"I guarantee I will get to every little spot on you, before the night is over. I just want to fulfill your every dream."

Slowly, he removed the silky fabric from her shoulders. Roxie murmured his name as she arched her back bringing her breast ever so close to his awaiting lips. Like a well-choreographed dance, they melded into each other, each one moving into the other.

Her skin was dewy and damp, and glistened in the candlelight. Bringing her breast to him, he licked the rise above her bra, tasting the salty moisture. Roxie's nipples protruded fiercely through the lace of her bra, as he continued to taste her skin. Her breathing made her chest rise and fall to his beckoning.

With one quick flip of his fingers, the hook of her bra was loosened, allowing her full breasts to explode from the confining fabric holding them in. Boothe's strong hands kneaded them carefully as he sucked the dark pink nipples that perked to perfection making her skin look even creamier.

As Boothe whispered her name, and sweet sounds of love to her, she begged him to take more. Roxie removed his shirt quickly and wiggled free of the binding fabric of the pantsuit she so painstakingly had chosen to wear for him. She ran her hands up his well-defined back, caressing his shoulder blades, and enjoying the shocking smoothness of his skin. Her fingers skimmed along his sides making him shudder with just the slightest bit of ticklishness. She found it endearing that such a strong man could be sent into that aspect of childishness, by just a simple touch.

Her fingers continued to glide around his abdomen and up into the rich mat of hair on his chest. Roxie loved the feel of his hot flesh up against hers. Slowly, her tongue found his erect nipple. She flicked it gently, making him moan her name.

"Roxie," he whispered, "God, Roxie, I want to be gentle with you, but I don't know how much more I can take."

Roxie slid her hands under the waistband of his pants.

"No skivvies?" Roxie asked him.

"I don't wear skivvies when I'm at home."

"Oh my," she said as she sat up. She pulled off his pants and brought him close to her with her hands surrounding his buttocks.

Her eyes went wide when she saw the size of him. Roxie smiled approvingly as she finished undressing him.

"Damn, Boothe. You were obviously worth waiting for," she said, as she firmly grabbed hold of his erection, making his juices trickle slightly out of the opening that yearned to spill more into her.

Boothe knelt down to her and let his fingers skim down her legs as he removed the thigh high stockings she wore. His hands, shaking with desire for her body, found their way to her slick and inviting cunt.

"Darlin', you really are ready for me, huh?" he said as he slid her panties down, to fall quietly to the floor.

"Um hmm," she replied as she continued to rub the nub of her arousal against his thick cock. Roxie eased across to her nightstand and opened the top drawer. It amazed him that she could even make the action of sliding on a condom excruciatingly sexy.

The wanting she felt for him left tears welling up in her eyes as she pulled his shaft closer to her. He pulled her hips up toward him and thrust himself gently inside her. She would have squealed except his mouth completely covered hers, as their bodies moved in perfect rhythm to their beating hearts. Instead, Roxie moaned and sighed deeply as the grand size of his cock completely filled and satisfied her.

Together they raced over the edge. Thrusting move by move with each other, Roxie squeaked slightly, as she peaked to his cock pulsating inside her pussy.

They lay perfectly still except for the loud pounding of their heartbeats in their chests, and the gasps of breath that continued to find their normal rhythm. That was perfectly acceptable, neither one of them wanted to move.

Boothe experienced good sex and even great sex before, but that's all it was...sex. This was a feeling he had never experienced. The complete letting go of all composure, to give, and take, the extreme pleasure, of true lovemaking. This was a feeling that until this moment he never felt before. Realizing he must be burying her in the mattress, Boothe began to lift himself off her.

"If you move, I'm going to have to hurt you," Roxie said as she grabbed him by the buttocks, squeezing slightly.

"Rox, I was just trying to move off of you before I hurt you," he said, as he started to laugh.

"I'm fine. I don't want you to go anywhere," she said as she left small kisses across his chest. "Boothe, I never knew that sex could be like this. I want more."

"Can I rest a minute, Rox?" Boothe said as he tried to pretend she hadn't worn him to a frazzle.

"Wasn't it you who said we may not even like each other afterwards?" Boothe said as he slowly slid down her a bit so he could look into her eyes.

"This wasn't just sex, Roxie. I knew that being with you would be good, but I just didn't know how good. This was something much more than just a good ol' romp in the hay."

Boothe leaned down and gave Roxie a very tender and loving kiss. It was then she knew she was in love with him.

Boothe rolled over on his back pulling Roxie on top of him. He ran his thumbs over her nipples making them spring to attention before he suckled them. Gasping slightly, Roxie bent down to him and began running her tongue softly over each of his nipples. Before she realized it, she had the tiny nub between her teeth tugging ever so gently.

"God, Roxie," Boothe called as he dug his fingers into her back. "That feels incredible."

She liked pleasing him so she continued her trail of nibbles and kisses across his hairy chest, and up his neck. She loved the way the dark hair covered his chest and stomach entirely and worked its way down to a full mass between his thighs.

Roxie could feel his arousal begin again as he rose up against her stomach. She looked at him seductively, raising an eyebrow in question, stirring his blood once again.

"Should I grab another suit of armor for my warrior?"

Grabbing her neck, Boothe pulled her into him. They continued where the dance before had ended, moving into each other in a continuous motion, bringing them both to the peak of craziness. Boothe loved the expressions that came over her face when she was in complete ecstasy.

He held her face in his hands as their eyes locked and they came together once again.

Roxie got up eventually and went into the bathroom to wash up and take off her makeup, that was now stinging her eyes. She barely heard the quiet rap on the door.

"I'm sorry, Roxie," Boothe said as he came in shutting the door behind him, "but I gotta go."

Roxie smiled at the way Boothe had no qualms about relieving himself in front of her.

"By all means, help yourself," she said a bit shocked.

When Boothe returned to the bedroom he began putting his pants on and gathering up the rest of his clothes.

"You're not going, are you?"

"I didn't know if you wanted me to stay all night because of Aaron. It's your call."

"I want you to stay," she told him as she got into bed. "I'll keep the bed warm for you," she said with a welcoming smile as she turned the covers back.

Sometime later they lay together silently, soaking in the other's warmth. Boothe lay on his back with Roxie nestled in on his chest, running her fingers through the hairs that covered him. *It doesn't get much better than this,* he thought to himself.

Her body was soft and warm and he loved the feel of it up against him. Roxie's breathing began to ease back to normal, as she closed her eyes to enjoy the moment. Her stomach began to grumble and he smiled and kissed the top of her head.

"Wanna raid the fridge?" Roxie asked him.

"I was just thinking the same thing. We did burn a few calories, wouldn't you say?"

As Roxie crawled over Boothe, he grabbed her buttocks with his hands and squeezed them tightly.

"Holy shit, Roxie. What is this on your ass?"

Roxie blushed remembering her tattoo. The symbol of her only act of rebellion shortly after her divorce was final. A butterfly to represent freedom.

"I…uh…a butterfly."

"Well, fuck me."

"I believe I already did."

"I mean, I would never have thought you would have a tattoo. You're so wholesome and all," Boothe said rubbing his hands across her ass.

"You're so soft and round. I can't control myself from grabbing onto you."

"I thought you were hungry?" she asked when she finally broke away from him to put on a t-shirt.

"I am but I wanted to enjoy the scenery first. I've waited a long time to see you naked. Now I just want to enjoy it."

"Don't put a shirt on," she told him as she sidled out the door. "I love looking at your chest."

"Hey, come here," he said pulling her toward him, before scooping her up in his arms.

"Why are you always picking me up and carrying me someplace? You're gonna hurt your back."

"You don't weigh enough to hurt my back. Besides, I already told you I can't keep my hands off of you. Now that I know what you look like under your clothes, it's gonna be that much harder for me to stop from ravishing you in public."

Roxie slid down the front of him when they got to the kitchen.

"How about a cold meatball sandwich and big ol' glass of milk?"

Boothe was the first one to wake. He basked in the afterglow of their evening together. *Four times.* God, he had never made love to a woman four times in one night. He stood in the bathroom doorway, watching her as she smiled in satisfaction, as she rolled over across the bed.

He loved her. He didn't know how or when it happened, but the fact remained. He was absolutely head over heels, hopelessly, pathetically, in love with her.

The scary part was that he loved the kid, too. God, if anyone had told Boothe O'Brien that he would be a father, he would have laughed in their faces. The kid made him melt when he grabbed him by the legs and called his name.

Shit! What the hell was he going to do now?

She stretched fully and got up to head downstairs when she felt the soreness that spread through her crotch. *You are a slut,* she said to herself. *It's a wonder you can walk at all.*

The hunger of wanting spread through his loins when she emerged from the stairs. He stood in awe, staring at her as she smiled innocently, approaching him wearing a skimpy white t-shirt over flannel boxers.

The sun beaming through the glass bricks at the front of the house lit the copper and auburn tones in her hair to a fiery glow. She flipped a long strand of sleep-tousled hair out of her eyes, and tried to focus on him.

"Good morning," she said yawning. She stretched her arms over her head making the dark skin around her nipples beckon him through the thin cotton of her shirt.

Boothe's arousal pulsated now as his sweat pants tented with his erection. She looked no older than twelve standing there looking at him. Shocking him back to reality, his hard-on diminished when he thought of her that way. He noticed that it seemed difficult for her to walk across the room to him.

Roxie tried not to show that the movement of her thighs moving across each other shot pain into her abdomen that she knew was worse than labor pains. She smiled unconvincingly at Boothe, noticing the concern spread across his face.

"Damn, Roxie. I'm sorry," he said as he came to her pulling her into him. "I didn't mean to hurt you."

"It was well worth it," she said smiling, "but you should register that thing of yours as an assault weapon."

Roxie loved making him blush. The dark shadow of stubble couldn't hide the redness that spread across his face.

Making their way to the sofa, Boothe sat down and then carefully pulled her down to him. She straddled him, moaning slightly as she spread her legs around his hips. Kissing him gently on the lips, Roxie could feel him hardening quickly under her. She laid her head on his bare chest running her fingers through the dark fur that covered his chest.

"I love being with you like this," she told him, as she purred slightly when he squeezed her tightly up against him.

"There's somethin' I need to say to you, Roxie."

Before he could continue, Roxie's heart began to thump hard as if it would beat out of her chest. Was this it? Was he going to tell her that last night was great, but...? She couldn't take being rejected by him.

"It's all right, Boothe. I know. We had a great night last night, but that's all it was and will be. I'm not holding you to anything, so don't worry."

"No, no, Roxie. You've got the wrong idea. Last night was wonderful and I don't want it to end."

They both startled at the sound of the doorbell.

Chapter Twelve

"God, Nikki. What's wrong?" Roxie yelled spying the tears pouring down her cousin's face when she opened her front door.

"Rox, Will is coming home!" Nikki screamed as Boothe ran around the corner of the hallway.

"Nikki, shit. I thought something was wrong with the baby or Aaron," Boothe said with a slight quiver in his voice. "I gotta sit down," he said grabbing the chair by Roxie's telephone table.

"Aw, Boothe. You do have a heart, don't you?" Nikki asked him as she kissed him on the cheek. She placed Aaron in his arms.

Boothe softened at the feeling of Nikki's tears on his face. "You just kind of scared me, that's all."

"I didn't mean to scare either one of you. I am just so freakin' excited I can't stand it!" Nikki said as she hugged Roxie tightly. "Besides, y'all look kind of funny…Wait a minute…I know that look. You got nasty last night, didn't you? Oh…my…God! You did, Roxie. You're blushing. Holy shit, Boothe! You're blushing, too! Wait 'til I tell Will about this…" Nikki continued as she let herself out.

Roxie and Boothe could hear her giggling as she walked back home. Looking at each other, they too began to snicker.

"I guess we do look kind of guilty, huh?" Roxie asked Boothe.

"Just a bit, I imagine."

"Boo, you nasty?" The toddler asked him as he cupped his face with his tiny hands.

"Only with your momma, munchkin."

* * * * *

The smell of parmesan, marinara, garlic, and onions filled their noses when the foursome entered the quaint Italian restaurant in the heart of downtown Harrogate. This was to be a night of celebration. A celebration of a soldier coming home, one life created by two, and two hearts becoming one.

Both men entered with the loves of their lives on their arms. One knew it, and practically puffed out with pride. The other was scared shitless to admit it, even to himself.

Will smiled at his friend. It wasn't too very long ago when he walked in his shoes. In love so deep that he knew he would never get out. However, now he knew that he never wanted to. Nikki was everything he ever wanted. Now, carrying his child, it took all the strength any Marine had not to burst into tears whenever he saw her. Being pregnant made her even more beautiful, if that was even possible.

Boothe had never had this pain in his chest when a woman looked at him. Roxie gave it to him. Just the smell of her wafting by him caused his heart to race and his blood to pump at full speed in his chest. He had done it. He had lost his heart to her. Was there any way of going back? Did he want to? Hell, no. Roxie McNamara replaced anything that pretended to fulfill him in the past. Roxie and that little boy...God, he loved them. That's what the pain was. He loved them and they needed to know.

Will and Nikki sat quietly enjoying the show. Boothe sat, mouth agape as Roxie, completely oblivious, draped a long strand of spaghetti across her tongue. His mouth watered as she seductively sucked the strand through her wet lips.

"Gorgeous, you gotta stop that or else I'm going to throw you across this table and pump you right here in public," Boothe said trying to regain his composure.

Shocked, Roxie looked at him, and then at Will and Nikki. Both snickered.

"What are you talking about, Boothe?" Roxie drawled in her most innocent Southern Belle style.

"You know exactly what I'm talking about, Roxie. Shit, I have created a monster. But, damn, I love it," Boothe said pulling Roxie into him, kissing the top of her head.

Without thinking Roxie slid her hand between Boothe's thighs under the table. Slowly her hand traced the form of his hard shaft pressing tightly against the zipper of his pants. She felt him start at her touch. She continued pressing the palm of her hand down the length of him as his erection hardened with each touch of her fingertips.

Roxie was surprised at her release of inhibitions. Never, ever, had she touched John's dick in public, nor had she wanted to, but she did now. Even though she knew no one saw what she was doing under the table, she figured Will and Nikki were aware of her, from Boothe's glazed-over look.

"Dude, you okay?" Will asked Boothe, snickering.

Coughing slightly, Boothe sat up straight in his seat. "Yea, I'm just dandy."

Boothe leaned into Roxie and whispered in her ear, "You are gonna get your brains fucked out when we get home."

It could have been the wine, but Roxie was sure that it was the man that made her whisper in reply, "Not if I fuck you here first."

Everyone at the table could see the sweat pop up across Boothe's brow. "Okay, I surrender. Take me. Do whatever you want," Boothe said holding his hands up.

"All in good time, my love," Roxie replied, kissing him firmly on the mouth. "We haven't had dessert yet."

"Shit, I don't know if I can make it through dessert."

* * * * *

Roxie's nails scraped across Boothe's chest as she ripped his shirt off him. Boothe stared in shock at the sound of the fabric ripping at the seams.

"Shit, Roxie. What has gotten into you?"

"You have gotten into me, Boothe O'Brien. Don't you know that?" she replied kissing the mat of hair in the center of his chest. Roxie let her tongue be her guide to each of his nipples, and then up over his Adam's apple, and finally to his hot mouth. "You make me feel like a woman," she said tracing around his mouth with her tongue. "You make me feel like I am the only woman in the world when I am with you," she said, as she feathered kisses across his lashes.

Roxie's throat burned and she could feel the tears sting her eyes. Never had she experienced feelings like this. Boothe had her heart. It tore her up to think of him leaving her. But, she knew he would someday. Boothe was not one to commit to any woman. She knew that from the beginning. She told herself she could live with that. However, now that she had experienced the pleasure of Boothe O'Brien, she didn't know if she could ever go back to the woman she once had been. God help her. She wanted to belong to him.

She decided right then, she would make him love her.

She pulled at his nipples with her teeth making him moan with pleasure.

"Roxie, you feel so good," Boothe said as he pressed her head into his chest.

The dewy head of his cock rubbed between her breasts as she continued to run her tongue across every inch of his body. Roxie scraped her nails down the small of his back. Her fingers traced the soft skin of his buttocks until she felt his shiver overtake him. Roxie smothered his cock with her breasts. Her skin was so soft there as she firmly sandwiched them together, rubbing up and down the length of his thick cock.

Boothe's breath hitched slightly, as he enjoyed the feel of her rubbing the length of him.

"I've never had anyone come all over me, Boothe. I want you to do that. I want to feel how much you want me," Roxie said as she pressed her breasts up and down, faster until he could no longer hold back the climax that overtook him.

"Yes, Roxie. Smear my come all over your beautiful body. Paint yourself with me."

She smoothed his sticky ejaculate over her breasts as he continued to pump his seed out of the head of his cock. Roxie ran her hands down to her throbbing pussy and spread his juices over her bulging clit.

"Boothe, I want to come. Please make me come," she said as she lowered his head down to her.

"Spread your legs, baby. I want to taste how horny you are for me."

Boothe licked her clit with such desire that just a few flicks of his tongue made her writhe with her own orgasm. He drank in all the juices escaping her. His tongue circled the softness as it entered her. Her buttocks pressed into the pillows as she crumpled the sheets in her hands.

"Oh, God. Boothe, you feel so good."

"No one feels as good as you, gorgeous," Boothe said holding her until her heartbeat stabilized once again.

Chapter Thirteen

"I don't want to hurt you," Will said attempting to hold his passion for his wife in check.

"You're not going to hurt me. At least not in a bad way," Nikki said as she pulled at Will's shirt.

"What if something happens to the baby?"

"Nothing is going to happen, Will. The doctor said it was okay."

"You promise?" Will said as he ran kisses up and down Nikki's neck.

"I promise, now get over here and have your way with me."

"That's all I want to do."

Will ran his hands over his wife's belly that now encased his child. "You have never been sexier to me than you are right now," he told Nikki, as he continued caressing her softly.

Nikki ran her hands up Will's chest and grabbed hold of his face. "You, Will Chambers, are sex deprived and delirious."

"Sex deprived, yes. Delirious, no. Now, get your ass over here so I can ravage you," he said pulling her into him.

Nikki's swollen breast filled his mouth as he suckled her protruding nipple.

"I have missed you so much, darlin'," Will said as he continued to cover her body with hot kisses. Not one inch of flesh did he pass up. Months had passed since he had touched her. He had a lot of making up to do.

Nikki grabbed his buttocks, squeezing tightly while pulling him into her. As she lay on her back, Will spread her legs gently, opening her wet pussy up to him. His tongue toured the soft flesh of her clit that had for so long been neglected. Nikki arched into Will, as her body shuddered with every flick of his tongue. Only seconds passed before the first of many orgasms overtook her. She gasped in ecstasy with each convulsion of release.

Will held his thick shaft, guiding it into her gently. They moaned in unison at the sheer pleasure of feeling each other again. Carefully, he pushed his throbbing cock deeper into her slick pussy. They moved together in rhythm, each person accepting what the other was giving.

Nikki wrapped her legs around Will's waist, pulling him that much deeper into her beckoning pussy. The climax took them both by such force, they yelped with excruciating pleasure that left them both heaving for air.

"God, I've missed feeling you inside me," Nikki said stroking the taut muscles running down his abdomen. "I forgot how incredible you feel."

"You should be on my end. You can't imagine what it feels like to have you wrapped around me so tightly. It is the most indescribable feeling I have ever had. I love you, Nik."

"Oh my God!" she said as she placed her hand on the slight swell of her belly.

"What is it? I told you I was afraid of hurting you," he said in a panic.

"No, sweetie. I'm not hurt. Your baby is moving. I can feel a little flutter inside. I haven't felt that before now. I think it's saying, 'Welcome home, Soldier'."

* * * * *

"Don't pay any attention to him. He's just showing off for you. I don't have the strength to make love to you again right now, no matter what he thinks. God, I can't believe those words even passed out of my mouth. I must be getting old," Boothe said laughing as he cradled Roxie against his chest.

Roxie smiled up into his dark eyes, the same dark eyes that had captivated her heart and her soul.

"That's a good thing. Otherwise, I don't know that I would be able to walk tomorrow."

* * * * *

Boothe thought he was dreaming. Make that having a nightmare. That was, until he lay on Roxie's bed, wide awake, and was still able to hear the screeching sound coming from down the hall. Roxie was no longer lying next to him in the bed. Surely to God that wasn't her making that horrendous noise?

Boothe followed the howling sound into Roxie's bathroom. God love her. That sound was coming from her. How could someone so beautiful have such a hideous singing voice? You couldn't even call it singing. She sounded like a wounded animal, howling in agony. Whatever she was trying to sing was unrecognizable.

"Uh, Roxie. Are you okay?" Boothe asked her as he peeped his head inside the shower curtain.

"Yea, why?" she asked him, trying to cover herself with the washcloth she used.

"I hate to break it to you, gorgeous, but you sounded like you were dying in here." Despite the fact that her singing made him cringe the view of her wet and soapy in the shower, still took his breath away. "Why don't you let me give you something to do besides sing," he said as he slipped into the shower behind her.

"I know I can't sing, but I love to. I forgot it wasn't just me and Aaron here this morning. Sorry."

"You are going to warp that kid for life if you sing like that every morning," he said, as he ran the washcloth over her breasts. "Here, I have something else for your mouth to do," he said as he covered her lips with his.

Roxie ran her hands over his firm chest muscles letting the soap lather in the mass of hair that covered him. She traveled down to his cock that was already extremely hard, and ready to thrust into her.

"My, oh my. I do declare you have the largest appendage I have ever seen," Roxie teased in an exaggerated Southern drawl. "I think I might swoon."

She squeaked with delight as Boothe pressed her back firmly against the bathroom tiles. His mouth found each breast and then moved down her belly to the red curls that covered her pussy, now ablaze with desire.

Boothe spread the lips of her cunt, parting the silky red hairs in the process. He held his cock in his hand and pushed it into her deeply.

"Hold me," she cried as she locked her hands behind his neck.

Boothe grabbed hold of her silky buttocks as she wrapped her legs around him. He pumped into her again and again, as she rocked with his rhythm. The water beat down on them, as they came in one immense climax. Boothe fought hard to control the weakness in his knees so not to cause them both to fall out of the shower.

"God, you really are amazing. You know that?" Boothe asked her as his cock slipped out of her pussy. His juices slithered down her inner thighs. Looking down at herself, she saw the tell-tale signs of his condom that remained inside her.

"You look like one of those balloon machines," Boothe said trying to make light of the situation.

"All I know is that I need another shower," Roxie replied biting his bottom lip playfully. "You wash my back and I'll wash yours."

Chapter Fourteen

Roxie walked into her classroom of wide-eyed first graders. The first day of school always thrilled her. She loved the smell of new paint, new books and new clothes.

When she and her class returned from lunch, Roxie spotted a huge box of chocolates in the middle of her desk. There was a pink envelope lying on top with her name written on the outside. Her stomach fluttered as she opened the envelope.

Hope you have a great day, Teach.
Maybe if you save some of these we can do
something highly "unscholarly" with them later.
Love, Boothe

He had actually signed it "Love, Boothe". She wondered if he actually meant it, or was that what he wrote to all the women he wooed. Who really gave a shit? The fact was that for no matter how brief of a moment, she was on his mind long enough to buy and deliver a sweet token of thoughtfulness for her first day at a new school. God knew John would never think of such a thing.

What in the hell happened to him? He swore he just had an out of body experience. He vaguely remembered buying the card and chocolates at the Base Exchange. He then snuck into her classroom, like a kid trying to steal quiz answers, and placed them on her desk. He knew if he saw her, he would make more of a fool of himself than he already had. Her scent lingering in the classroom was enough to make his libido go into fast forward mode anyway. He could try to avoid it all he wanted to, but he knew the truth. He was madly in love, for the first time in his life, and he didn't know how he was going to handle it.

Someone knocked on Boothe's door just as he got out of the shower.

"Yea, hang on a minute," he yelled wrapping a towel around his waist.

"Is that you, Roxie?"

He opened the door to Louise Shafer. Boothe once enjoyed the things this woman could do to a man especially when enough booze was down the both of them. His eyes roamed over the length of her. Old habits die hard. Besides she did have one of the best bodies money could buy and liked flaunting it. Funny thing was, she didn't do it for him. Boothe was truly disappointed as he opened the door to Louise when he hoped it was Roxie.

Without warning, Louise pushed Boothe up against the doorjamb, and proceeded to rub her body all over his.

"So, O'Brien, who the hell is Roxie?" she asked him just a breath away from his mouth.

"That would be me," a voice came up behind her, startling them both.

Never before had Boothe felt the dread of being caught in a compromising position with another woman. However, his stomach hit his feet as he waited for Roxie's response to this untimely moment.

"Louise, this is Roxie McNamara," Boothe said uneasily.

"Let me guess, honey. Are you the flavor of the day?" Louise sneered at Roxie. "She's a little innocent for your tastes isn't she, Boothe, darling?"

"Well, Louise, my tastes have changed a lot since the last time we were together," he said, as he reached out to put his arm around Roxie's waist and pull her into his side. Tightly.

"Whatever. You know where to find me when you get tired of little Miss Prim and Proper," Louise purred as she ran a fingertip across his chest from one nipple to the other.

Boothe tilted her chin up to look at him. "I'm sorry, Rox."

"I guess she is one your harem, huh?"

"Was, Roxie. It was a long time ago and I was very drunk. I know that's not an excuse, but it is the truth."

"It's just hard to see someone that I know you've done the things with that you do to me." She was finding it hard to meet his eyes.

"Roxie, don't you ever compare yourself to any of them. You are the most incredible woman I have ever been with. You have turned my life completely upside down. I don't even know who I am anymore. "

"I'm sorry, Boothe. I didn't mean to do any such thing," Roxie said pulling away from him and walking into his barracks.

"It's a good thing, Roxie. You are taking this completely wrong. What I'm trying to say is…that…I think I love you."

Roxie turned around abruptly, in complete shock.

"Did you really say that?"

"Yea, I did. Trust me. I didn't even think those words could even be uttered by me, Rox. See what you've done? I'm completely whooped!"

Roxie flopped down on his sofa, still unable to speak. In her heart she knew Boothe saying those words to her, was probably the toughest thing he had ever done. Gaining her composure, she stood up and walked over to Boothe. Slowly, she brought her hand up to his cheek.

"Boothe, I think I know the man that you are. You had me wrapped up in you the first time you picked up my son. I was once married to someone who never made me or Aaron feel the way you do. I love you right back, Boothe. I didn't think I'd ever find love again. You have changed me, too."

Boothe grabbed her and covered her mouth with his. On a guttural groan he slipped his tongue between her lips. The towel that covered him fell to the floor and his erect cock pressed against her stomach.

"Make love with me, Boothe. I want you so badly," she said in a whisper.

His deft fingers quickly removed her clothing. Carefully, he lay her down on the carpet. Boothe covered her body with light nips from his teeth, while she moaned incessantly. Her rapid heartbeat made him hunger for more of her.

Boothe's heart literally ached with desire, as her skin melted into his. Unable to contain himself any longer, he thrust his thick shaft into her. Roxie's slick pussy sheathed him tightly. Her nails dug into the skin on his shoulder blades making him pump her harder. As his orgasm reached the boiling point she screeched with her own climax.

"I've never given any chick a carpet burn on their ass before. I'm really sorry for burning your ass on the carpet, Rox," Boothe said as he spread medicated cream across the deep red lines, crossing the butterfly, on her buttocks.

"How would you know? Correct me if I'm wrong, but did Love 'em and Leave 'em Boothe O'Brien ever stick around to see what happened to them the next morning?" Roxie teased him.

"Uh, maybe not."

"Don't fret any, Boothe. I enjoyed every minute of pain," she said wincing at the touch of his fingers.

"Uh, gorgeous, I think I need to take a cold shower," he said looking down at the bulge growing quickly between his legs.

"Good God, Boothe. Is there nothing that doesn't turn you on?"

"If there is, I sure as shit don't know what it is. Face it, Rox. You are hot no matter what you are doing, saying, wearing, or whatever. Just the thought of you makes my dick hard. Don't you know that?"

"I guess so," Roxie said blushing. "I'm going to need better vitamins."

Chapter Fifteen

"Okay, dude. Spill it," Will said as he bent over to ignite the grill. "What exactly are your intentions with Roxie?"

"I'm in love with her."

"What did you say?"

"You heard me, asshole. I'm in love with her and the kid. What in the fuck happened to me, huh?" Boothe said, drawing deeply from the beer bottle he held.

"You're shitting me, right? I didn't think love was in your vocabulary."

"Yea, well neither the fuck did I."

"What do you think they're talking about out there?" Nikki asked Roxie.

"Us. Don't they just look precious?" Roxie said biting her lip.

"Fuck, Roxanne. You are in fucking love. Aren't you?"

"Yes," Roxie said unable to stifle the giggle that bubbled up in her throat. "You know what's really going to scare the shit out of you? Boothe's in love with me, too. He told me last night."

"Holy shit. I've got to sit down. Our Boothe actually uttered those exact words to you?"

"Yes, Nikki. I couldn't believe it myself, but he did." Roxie drained the wine in her glass and beamed down at her cousin.

"You can thank me later for hooking you two up. Rub my ankles, will you? They're the size of an elephant's."

* * * * *

"Well, well, you must be the Marine pussy who's fucking my whore of a wife," the drunken voice came across the telephone line, when Boothe answered.

"I told Roxanne I have no problems flying over there to kick your sorry ass," John yelled at Boothe. "When I'm through with you, I'll take care of that cunt next. It'll be a long time before anyone will want to even look at her. Now, grunt, put the bitch on the phone."

Panic covered Roxie's face when she noticed Boothe's changed expression. The fury in his eyes frightened her. She was sure only one person could cause such a reaction from Boothe.

John McNamara.

"First of all, you sorry excuse for a dick, if you want to kick my ass, bring it on. What I hear is you prefer to beat the shit out of women, around five feet eight and one hundred and ten pounds. I'm afraid I don't exactly fit that description, you cock sucker," Boothe yelled back, trying to regain his composure. There was no way in hell he would let an asshole like John McNamara think he was getting the best of him.

"Just for the record, you pussy, Roxie is not your wife anymore. Fact is, she would be mine if you hadn't fucked up her mind so bad. If you ever call here again and harass her, I will fly my ass to Texas and beat you like you deserve. No one will miss you and they will never find your sorry corpse!" Boothe slammed the phone back on the receiver, and turned to Roxie.

She rocked back and forth on the bed, tears rolling down her cheeks.

"Aw, sweetie, don't cry. I could tear his fucking heart out for what he's done to you," Boothe said taking Roxie in his arms. "I meant what I said about taking care of you and Aaron. You don't have to worry about him ever hurting you again."

"I can't believe I wasted my life with him. Aaron is the only thing good to come out that horrendous marriage. There is still a lot I haven't told you, but if I spill my guts, I don't want to ever bring it up again, okay?" Roxie asked him.

"Okay, gorgeous, whatever you want."

"He put on a great show. Everyone thought he was wonderful and that we were the perfect couple. However, behind the scenes he was controlling, abusive and extremely jealous. The drunker he was, the worse he got.

"I was a virgin when we married. He liked knowing that he was my first and only. Unfortunately, I didn't hold the same position for him. I don't know when the cheating began, but I became aware of it shortly after we were married." Roxie turned to look at Boothe and then quickly looked away.

"One time, he wanted to 'borrow' his buddy's wife. I wouldn't have anything to do with it, so he blacked my eye. Every time I got up enough nerve to leave, he would come groveling back and I would forgive him.

"I thought when I got pregnant it would be a wake up call for him. At first, he hid the fact that he continued to screw around. Eventually, he didn't even try to hide it. The end was when he tried to rape me when I was more than eight months pregnant," Roxie began sobbing.

Boothe rubbed her back, allowing her to purge the emotions she held in for far too long. A few moments later, Roxie continued to tell Boothe her story.

"I went home until Aaron was born. He showed up at the hospital saying he had joined AA. He told me he wanted to raise his son, and that he would never hurt me again. I soon found out it was all a bunch of lies. I came home from school one day finding him, and his boss, screwing in our bed. He actually asked me to watch them, and learn. He was such a sick son of a bitch. That's when I left and never went back."

"After the divorce, he tried to use Aaron to get to me. He threatened to take me to court and prove I was an unfit mother. He told me he had friends in high places that would swear to anything he asked them to. I finally decided I had to get far away from him. So here I am."

Boothe pulled her close to him. Never before had he felt the desire to rip another human being apart with his bare hands. However, John McNamara was not exactly human.

"You are the only one who knows everything. I couldn't even tell Nikki, because I was too embarrassed. I love you, I want you to know where I have been, and how it made me the woman I am now," Roxie said while tears continued streaming down her cheeks.

"You know, Roxie. I meant it when I said I want to marry you. I never thought I would want that. Just the idea made my skin crawl. But, if we were married, you could get rid of that sorry piece of shit forever."

"Boothe, I don't want to marry you just to get rid of John. If we get married, it's because we love each other," Roxie said pressing her cheek into his chest.

"Well, don't we?" Boothe questioned her.

"Yes, but everything has gone so fast. I want to enjoy every moment spent with you. Just give me a little more time to adjust being the 'one-and-only' for the infamous, Boothe O'Brien. Okay?"

"I won't pressure you, Roxie. But, don't make me wait too long, huh?" Boothe said as he held her tighter.

* * * * *

The guys were thirty minutes late. Nikki and Roxie attempted to avoid the fact that something felt wrong by playing with Aaron in his high chair, as they awaited their arrival at the club restaurant on base. Their feelings were validated when the two men entered the doorway.

"What's wrong?" they asked in unison.

"We've been ordered to go on an emergency security mission. Gunny says we should be in and out, two weeks tops," Will said unconvincingly.

"But, what about..." Nikki blurted.

"It's okay, darlin'. The baby's not due for four weeks. I'll be back in plenty of time. Don't worry your pretty little head about it, okay?" Will said as he stroked the side of Nikki's face.

"So when are y'all leaving?" Roxie asked them.

"Right now. We have time to get our duffels packed, and that's it," Boothe replied.

"God, Boothe. Please don't try and be a hero. I love you."

"Yea, Gorgeous. I love you, too," he said blushing at Will and Nikki. "Why don't you use this time to think on what we talked about last night?"

"That's exactly what I plan on doing."

Chapter Sixteen

A week passed without one word from the men. Roxie and Nikki kept the news on, religiously trying to keep up to date on the military actions. As the tension increased, so did the tension of the women.

"Why don't you and Aaron spend the night with me?" Nikki asked Roxie. "I really don't feel like being alone."

"I know what you mean." Roxie replied holding back the tears that stung her eyes.

* * * * *

The screams of Nikki calling out to her, bolted her from her dreams. Roxie jumped up and ran to Nikki's room finding her doubled over on the bed, with the sheets twisted around her. As Roxie neared she noticed the pink tinge of the once white sheets.

"My water broke, Rox. What do I do?" Nikki asked her panting. "This wasn't supposed to happen yet. I'm scared, Roxie," Nikki cried.

"Everything's going to be fine, Nikki. Lay back and breathe deeply. I'm going to call your doctor, " Roxie said as she rubbed her cousin's back.

Once she got Nikki in the car, she ran to the house of the elderly couple next door. Mrs. Budd was always ready and willing to take care of Aaron, so Roxie got him settled with them before they left.

Roxie debated whether or not she should call Will's emergency number. Since there was nothing he could do at the moment and since her job was now to be Nikki's coach, she decided to call him after the delivery. Such is the life with a Marine. Will would have been here if there was any way possible. Shit, John was fucking his secretary while Roxie was having Aaron. Why couldn't she see what kind of man he was then?

"God, Roxie, he's beautiful," Nikki said as she beamed down at her newborn son. "He looks just like his daddy."

"It's always hard for me to tell when they are first born, exactly who they look like. He is beautiful though. You really did great, Nikki. Now, before I start crying again, I'm going home, get cleaned up, check on Aaron and call everybody. I'll be back later with your clothes and maybe even a cheeseburger, if you're a good girl." Roxie smiled down at Nikki and the baby.

"You really are an angel, Rox. I don't know what I would have done without you."

* * * * *

"What do you mean having the baby so early? Are you all right? Is he all right? I can't believe I wasn't there..." Will babbled to Nikki when he finally was able to call home.

"It's okay, Will. He's beautiful. We are both fine. Joshua really wants to meet his daddy," Nikki said smiling down at the bundle in her arms.

"God, Nik, you're going to make me cry. I hate that shit!"

Nikki gave a soft chuckle and called him Lt. Softy.

"Are you sure you are okay? I can't come home yet, you know?"

"I know. It's okay. Roxie is taking good care of us. We'll be waiting for you, so hurry home, okay?"

"I love you...I love you both."

* * * * *

Roxie was frazzled. She forgot how much dirty laundry a new baby produced. A mutual friend helped Nikki during the day and Roxie came over after work to take over.

"It's a sin that anyone can be skinnier than before she got pregnant just weeks after delivery," Roxie said teasing Nikki.

"Well, I wanted to be raring to jump Will's bones when they get home," Nikki said admiring herself in the mirror.

"Hold on, girlfriend. You are no way ready for a romp in the hay. You still have stitches. And do I need to remind you about that little pillow you carry around with you all the time?" Roxie said laughing. "The only one jumping anybody's bones, will be me!"

"Bitch!" Nikki said giggling. "You would have to rub it in."

"On that note, I'm going home. I need a long, hot bubble bath. You and Joshua are okay, aren't you?"

"Yea, we're fine. By the way," Nikki said shyly. "Have I told you lately how wonderful you are?"

"Only a billion times. I'm just glad that I was here to help. I'll see you tomorrow." Roxie said as she kissed Nikki on the cheek and Joshua on the crown of his downy soft, head.

Finally, Aaron was down for the night. Roxie endured hours of the toddler begging to go see his new baby, "Jo" as he so adorably called Joshua. Roxie made her way into the bathroom to run the hot water, when the doorbell startled her.

That better not be you, Nikki, Roxie said to herself.

She opened the door to looks of despair on Will and Nikki's face. Horror shot through her body. Nausea overtook her and Roxie swallowed hard to get rid of the bile rising in her throat. Black spots danced in front of her eyes and the light of the room narrowed in front of her face.

"Will, where's Boothe?" Roxie asked just before everything went black.

Chapter Seventeen

"Roxie, drink this," Nikki said handing her a jigger of dark brown liquid.

Roxie took a big gulp of the bourbon and stared horrified at Will.

"I'm going to be sick," Roxie said as she jumped up and ran to the bathroom to throw up.

She stood swaying in the doorway. Nikki gently led her to the couch and sat next to her, holding her hand.

"Roxie," Will said holding her chin up to look at him. "Boothe is not dead. I want to make that crystal clear. He was ordered to retrieve some documents and make it back to the designated rendezvous. Our orders were to leave at a specific time, whether all soldiers were back or not. If we hadn't left, Roxie, the whole mission would have been compromised. Boothe knows that."

"You just left him there?" Roxie asked, in shock. "He might be dead for all you know!"

"He's not. He's wearing a device that intelligence monitors, tracking his vital signs. They are attempting to track down his location, even as we speak. Another team will continue to observe the rendezvous site for Boothe until intelligence finds him, dead or alive."

"Oh, well, I feel much better now," Roxie said sarcastically.

"Look, Rox, he's going to be fine and be back home. I can guarantee Boothe O'Brien is too fucking stubborn to let some aggressor end it all for him. Especially, now that he has you and Aaron. That's enough to make any man fight for their life, with everything he's got. Don't worry. I swear, Roxie, I'll let you know anything as soon as I know. He's my best friend. I don't want anything to happen to him either." Will turned to the window so the women wouldn't see the fear in his eyes.

"It's just…things were just beginning for us, you know?" Roxie said, her hands trembling. "I was going to marry him."

"You still will, Rox," Nikki said, holding her tightly. "You still will."

* * * * *

Boothe jumped into the jeep, driven by an ally of the Marine Corps. About a mile from the designated site, all hell broke loose. Unbeknownst to Boothe and the driver, a sniper was waiting for them to appear. In one shot, a hole the size of a golf ball formed in the back of the guy's head. His reflexes caused his foot to press the gas all the way to the floor.

Hitting a dune, the jeep flipped four times before coming to a dead stop. Boothe lay under the jeep, in excruciating pain.

"Fuck, dude, you okay?" Boothe said, looking over at the driver to see that he definitely was anything but okay. Boothe wriggled free from the restraints, trying to ignore the shock of pain that ran from his right shoulder all the way down to his fingers.

Rolling along the sand as quickly as he could, Boothe made it into a bunker before the jeep exploded. The sky around Boothe filled with smoke, metal, and body parts. Boothe looked down to see blood pouring from the wound on his left leg. The gash must have been at least six inches long and two inches deep. Ripping his t-shirt apart he tied it around his upper thigh to stop the blood flow, just before he passed out.

* * * * *

"I fainted again didn't I," Roxie asked Colin Meriwether, the base physician.

"Two DOD men brought you in. Apparently, they were driving by just when you performed your graceful swan dive."

"Oh, great. I'm sure all of the base will be having a big laugh about this by dinner time," Roxie said rubbing her temples.

"You're awfully pale, Roxie. I am doing some blood work to make sure you're not anemic or anything. Now, would you like to tell me what's been going on with you?"

"I'm just a little run down that's all," Roxie said trying to convince herself, as much as Ian.

"I know that O'Brien is missing and I also know that you two are an item. A fact I am none too happy about, but that's another matter altogether. Have you been eating and sleeping well?"

"If you know about Boothe ,then you can answer that question yourself, I'm sure. I want to cry all the time. No, I don't want to eat, and I can't sleep. If I do manage to force something down, I usually end up tossing my cookies anyway. As soon as I know Boothe is alive and well, everything will be okay again."

"When was your last cycle, Roxie?"

"I'm not pregnant, Colin. I'm just stressed that's all."

"You can never be too sure, Roxie. I want you to take it easy for a few days, okay?"

"Okay, Ian, I'll try," Roxie said, before the door of the clinic bolted open.

"Roxie, are you okay?" Will asked worriedly.

"I'm fine. I think I just need to eat something."

"Is she free to go, Colin?" Will asked the doctor.

"Yes, but she has been ordered to rest for the next few days."

"Nikki and I will see to it she does exactly that."

Roxie roamed the aisles of the Base Exchange. Nothing sounded appetizing in the least. She filled her basket with Aaron's favorite crackers, fruit juice, two twelve-packs of Diet Coke, and two large bags of chocolates. Oh yes, and while she just happened to be on the feminine hygiene aisle, she'd pick up an EPT test.

When Roxie got back home, she read *Postman Pat* to Aaron until he finally went to sleep. Denying the pact she made with herself that he would always sleep in his own bed, she curled up next to him and soon slipped into a, desperately needed, slumber.

She awoke sometime in the middle of the night and remembered the pregnancy test she left on the bathroom counter. Slipping out of bed quietly, she tried not to wake her sleeping child. She walked, what seemed like a mile, to the bathroom just across the hall from her bedroom. Awaiting her arrival, the white stick beckoned her to see the results. Slowly, she lifted the stick to eye level, to view two pink dots.

Chapter Eighteen

Boothe awoke to the moaning and groaning of the military hospital. His blurred vision made it hard to focus on the surroundings, but he could hear the voices of the American caregivers around him.

His shoulder and leg throbbed like a beating drum. The pain almost making him sick to his stomach. He closed his eyes trying to focus on Roxie's face. She was all that occupied his mind since the accident. Was she frightened? Knowing her like he thought he did, she was probably making herself sick on chocolate and Diet Coke.

"Lieutenant, can you hear me?" the soft voice of a nurse questioned him.

"Yea," he said with the raspy voice of a dry throat. "Can I have some water?"

"Yes, sir. Right away," the nurse said pouring him a plastic cup full.

"Where am I?" Boothe asked.

"You're on board the Naval infirmary on its way back to England. Are you in any pain?"

"Fuck yea, I'm in pain. What the hell happened anyway?"

"You have a broken arm, shoulder, and you required thirty-two stitches in your upper thigh. You also had a minor concussion, that's why you've been out for a day or so."

"When do we dock in England?"

"I'd say, in about eight-and-a-half hours," the nurse said as she checked on the patient next to him.

God, he wanted to see Roxie. Nothing would be able to comfort him until he could hold her in his arms again. Then, all would be right with the world.

"Nurse, is there any way to use the phone around here?"

"Are you sure you're okay, man?" Will asked Boothe.

"Yea, just get her here as fast as you can. I need to see her."

"Will do, buddy. You just take care. We'll be there in a few hours."

✳ ✳ ✳ ✳ ✳

Roxie held onto Nikki as they walked past the injured in the hospital at RAF Lakenheath. She wasn't sure what to expect. Will told them he was okay, but was going to need medical attention for a few more days.

At the end of the hall, was the room marked, *O'Brien, B. Lt.* Will tapped on the door and awaited a response. There was none. He pushed the door open and looked in on a sleeping Boothe.

"It's okay, girls. He's just sleeping," Will said as he took Roxie by the arm.

Roxie made her way to Boothe's bedside. She took his hand in hers and kissed his forehead before sitting down in the nearest chair. His face was covered in a week's growth of beard. Even under the dark whiskers, she could see the handsomeness of his face. She stroked his temples, waiting anxiously for him to wake.

Will and Nikki sat at the end of the bed. The nurse came in twice to check his vitals before his eyes finally flickered with consciousness.

He could feel her warmth. Roxie's breath on his face comforted him. She squeezed his hand slightly and whispered his name.

"I'm here, sweetie. Can you wake up?" Roxie said fighting back tears.

His eyelids continued to flicker as he tried to focus on her face. If he could only see her, he would be okay. She leaned down to him and pressed a soft kiss against his lips. To her surprise, he kissed her back.

"So, will you marry me now?" he asked her in a raspy voice.

"Is this why you went off and got yourself hurt, so I would give in to you?" Roxie asked, her voice trembling.

"Yea, did it work?"

"Yes, Boothe O'Brien, it did. I don't ever want to be without you again."

Will and Nikki quietly stole out of the room to give them privacy. Before leaving the hospital, they stopped at the nurse's station.

"Room 214 is sleeping and his wife is staying with him tonight," he said raising his eyebrows in understanding.

"No problem, sir. We'll check on him in the morning," the young nurse replied.

Roxie carefully slid up on the hospital bed with him. Snuggling into him, she inhaled his scent, never wanting to forget what he smelled like. Her hand ran across his firm chest.

"I don't know what I would've done if you hadn't come back," Roxie whispered softly.

"I would've been dead if I didn't come back to you, Roxie. That's the only thing that will keep me away from you. So, how's the munchkin?"

"He's fine. He wants to see 'Boo' though. Mrs. Budd says that you are all he talks about."

Trying to get comfortable without causing Boothe any pain, Roxie accidentally placed her hand between his legs. His dick was hard as granite. Boothe snorted at her disgusted look.

"I want you so much, Roxie. Do me. Do me right here."

"Boothe O'Brien, I think that concussion was more than the doctors thought. Those nurses could come in here any minute."

"It's late at night. They will only come in here if I ring the buzzer. I'm not on my death bed, gorgeous."

"I can't believe I'm doing this," Roxie said, as she grabbed hold of his thick, hard shaft.

Boothe moaned with every touch. Using his good arm, he pulled her up to him slightly so he could access her full, pouty, mouth and kissed her feverishly.

Carefully, she pulled up the hospital gown to expose every long inch of his beckoning cock. Gently, Roxie impaled herself on his shaft. Rising up and down slowly, desperately afraid she would hurt him. Her pace and the heat in her cunt, caused his cock to harden even more. She could feel him tighten as she rode him. She paused, to look into his eyes and whispered, "I love you, Boothe."

Seconds later, they both went over the edge in a climax that took them both by surprise. Trying to catch her breath, she fell carefully on his chest, listening to the pounding of his heart.

"If that doesn't heal me nothing will."

Sliding down next to him she closed her eyes and they both fell to sleep. For the first time in a month, Roxie actually slept with no worries, and wrapped herself in dreams of love.

"Roxie," Nikki whispered the next morning, as she and Will opened Boothe's door. "Are you awake?"

"Hang on a sec. Don't let Will come in," Roxie replied, as she slid out of the bed.

Roxie straightened her clothes and turned to look at Boothe. He lay on the bed with the biggest smile spread across his face.

"I still can't believe you talked me into screwing in a hospital bed!" Roxie whispered to Boothe. "Okay. Y'all can come in."

Will and Nikki had met with Boothe's doctor before coming to his room. Discharge papers were being prepared so he could go home to finish recuperating. Will helped Boothe up to relieve himself in the bathroom. Roxie spied the huge gash that extended down his thigh. She gasped at the sight of it. Boothe winked at her, letting her know that it would heal and he would be okay.

Several minutes later, Boothe and Will emerged from the bathroom. Boothe was showered, shaved and dressed.

"Hey, dude, you're a pretty good wife, you know?" Boothe sneered at Will.

"Thanks, buddy. I was only trying to protect the nurses from the sight of your tool. You'd probably scare the shit out of the old crotchety nurse that is working the morning shift," Will replied leading Boothe back to his bed.

"Nikki, would you and Will see if Boothe's papers are ready?" Roxie asked giving them the signal that she needed to talk to Boothe privately.

"Sure, Rox, we'll be back in a few minutes."

As the two left the room, Boothe felt an anxiety that he couldn't explain. Roxie looked pale and scared. She sat down next to him on the bed and softly kissed his smooth shaven cheek.

"I need to tell you something, Boothe," Roxie said avoiding his eyes.

"Okay...is it bad news?" his dark eyes questioned her.

"I don't think so, but I'm not sure how you're going to take it."

The silence in the room was so thick you could cut through it with a knife. It seemed like hours before Roxie spoke again.

"I'm pregnant."

Boothe's mouth dropped as realization kicked in. A gasp of air expelled from his lungs as he looked down at Roxie.

"Wow, you're pregnant. I never thought…"

For the first time in history, Boothe O'Brien was speechless. He hobbled off the bed and limped across the room to the window to stare out over the parking lot. Moments later, a battered Boothe turned to look at Roxie, with his notorious grin on his face and muttered what sounded like, "Ooh Rah to the rug burn mambo."

"Well, you're going to have to marry me a little sooner than you expected, huh?"

Roxie crossed the room and embraced him carefully.

"So, you're okay with this?"

"Shit, Roxie. Why wouldn't I be? I have found the woman of my dreams, a fact that is a miracle in itself. She happens to have a fantastic kid who worships the ground I walk on. Now, we're going to have a child together. What more could a guy ask for? Especially one like me." Boothe pulled her into him and, for the first time in his memory, tears of love filled his eyes.

Epilogue

Eight months later, Roxie stood in front of the mirror staring at her swollen belly. The Marine Corps ball was the biggest function of the year. Nikki had spent weeks making sure this year would be the best ever. She had driven Roxie absolutely crazy with all the minute details.

The long silk black dress skimmed her hips and breasts with precision. Boothe entered the room and stood admiring his bride.

"God, you're beautiful," he said roaming over every inch of her with his eyes.

Gasping, Roxie brought her hand to her chest. "Speaking of beautiful, you are the most handsome man I have ever laid eyes on."

Every crease of his uniform was accented to perfection to flaunt the masculinity within. The man stood in all his glory, with the look of undying love across his face. Each button sparkled; each Medal of Honor twinkled down the front of his chest, accentuating the gleam in his dark eyes. Roxie's eyes traced the view from his starched collar down to the white belt that cinched his waist. Her eyes followed the red stripe of his pants to his spit shined shoes.

Boothe wanted his wife as much as he did that very first night. The swell of her belly only made him want her that much more. Inside, she protected the most precious gift. Not just one baby, but two. Who would have thought they would have twins? Not him, that's for sure. Hell, Boothe never thought he would ever be a father, yet here he was.

As she turned to him a smile spread across her face. She absolutely glowed as she stood with the light shining against her auburn hair. He walked to her and took her in his arms.

"Will was right. Pregnant women are the most beautiful."

"I think you and Will are warped. I'm not feeling very beautiful with your children break-dancing on my kidneys."

"I'd just as soon stay home and ravage your pregnant body all night long," Boothe said placing kisses up and down her slender throat.

"Oh, now that's a vision...Ow!...Uh oh..."

Just as the words left Roxie's mouth, her water broke.

"Nikki is going to kill me because it doesn't look like we're going to make the ball."

"Jesus, Rox. What is it with you and Nikki that you can't follow the rules? Nine months is supposed to mean nine months. You still have four weeks to go," Boothe yelled.

"Twins usually come early, Boothe. I guess I forgot to tell you that."

"Fuck, Roxie. I might have needed to know that info!"

Panicking, Boothe ran in the other room to call the doctor. Aggravated because his sword kept catching in the doorjamb, he ripped it off and threw it on the bed barely missing Roxie.

"There's no need to throw weapons, honey. We have plenty of time."

* * * * *

"God, Roxie. I can't believe the babies came so quickly," Nikki said as she entered Roxie's hospital room. "Where's the proud papa?"

"He won't let the nurses take the babies without him going, too. He is going to drive them crazy. He's so paranoid that someone is going to steal them!" Roxie said laughing. "He's a little freaked out that he is the father of four children under the age of three!"

"Four?" Will blurted out. "Did I miss something?"

Boothe entered the room pushing two bassinets with the nurse in tow, pushing another.

"The doctor was wrong. We had triplets, two girls and a boy. Will, Nikki...meet Catherine, Eliza and Bronson."

About the author:

The sensational mother/daughter writing team of Alli Nicole is comprised of Kris Fletcher and Judy Calvert.

Judy lives with her husband of thirty-four years in Florida. She has two daughters. Kris, her oldest daughter, is her writing partner.

Kris resides in North Texas with her husband and two children. In her spare time she enjoys reading, boating on the lake and spending time with her wonderful friends and family.

Alli welcomes mail from readers. You can write to her c/o Ellora's Cave Publishing at 1337 Commerce Drive, Suite 13, Stow OH 44224.

Why an electronic book?

We live in the Information Age—an exciting time in the history of human civilization in which technology rules supreme and continues to progress in leaps and bounds every minute of every hour of every day. For a multitude of reasons, more and more avid literary fans are opting to purchase e-books instead of paperbacks. The question to those not yet initiated to the world of electronic reading is simply: *why?*

1. *Price.* An electronic title at Ellora's Cave Publishing runs anywhere from 40-75% less than the cover price of the <u>exact same title</u> in paperback format. Why? Cold mathematics. It is less expensive to publish an e-book than it is to publish a paperback, so the savings are passed along to the consumer.

2. *Space.* Running out of room to house your paperback books? That is one worry you will never have with electronic novels. For a low one-time cost, you can purchase a handheld computer designed specifically for e-reading purposes. Many e-readers are larger than the average handheld, giving you plenty of screen room. Better yet, hundreds of titles can be stored within your new library—a single microchip. (Please note that Ellora's Cave does not endorse any specific brands. You can check our website at www.ellorascave.com for customer recommendations we make available to new consumers.)

3. *Mobility.* Because your new library now consists of only a microchip, your entire cache of books can be taken with you wherever you go.

4. *Personal preferences are accounted for.* Are the words you are currently reading too small? Too large? Too...**ANNOYING**? Paperback books cannot be modified according to personal preferences, but e-books can.

5. *Innovation.* The way you read a book is not the only advancement the Information Age has gifted the literary community with. There is also the factor of what you can read. Ellora's Cave Publishing will be introducing a new line of interactive titles that are available in e-book format only.

6. *Instant gratification.* Is it the middle of the night and all the bookstores are closed? Are you tired of waiting days—sometimes weeks—for online and offline bookstores to ship the novels you bought? Ellora's Cave Publishing sells instantaneous downloads 24 hours a day, 7 days a week, 365 days a year. Our e-book delivery system is 100% automated, meaning your order is filled as soon as you pay for it.

Those are a few of the top reasons why electronic novels are displacing paperbacks for many an avid reader. As always, Ellora's Cave Publishing welcomes your questions and comments. We invite you to email us at service@ellorascave.com or write to us directly at: 1337 Commerce Drive, Suite 13, Stow OH 44224.

Discover for yourself why readers can't get enough of the multiple award-winning publisher Ellora's Cave. Whether you prefer e-books or paperbacks, be sure to visit EC on the web at www.ellorascave.com for an erotic reading experience that will leave you breathless.

Printed in the United States
26965LVS00004B/70-489